BOW

Other Series by H.P. Mallory

Paranormal Women's Fiction Series:
Haven Hollow
Midlife Spirits
Midlife Mermaid

Paranormal Shifter Series:
Arctic Wolves

Paranormal Romance Series:
Underworld
Lily Harper
Dulcie O'Neil
Lucy Westenra

Paranormal Adventure Series:
Dungeon Raider
Chasing Demons

Detective SciFi Romance Series:
The Alaskan Detective

Academy Romance Series:
Ever Dark Academy

Reverse Harem Series:
Happily Never After
My Five Kings

BOWIE

Book 8
The Happily Never After Series

By

HP Mallory

10 Chosen Ones:
When a pall is cast upon the land,
Despair not, mortals,
For come forth heroes ten.
One in oceans deep,
One the flame shall keep,
One a fae,
One a cheat,
One shall poison grow,
One for death,
One for chaos,
One for control,
One shall pay a magic toll.

Chapter One
Bowie

I can't, for the life of me, figure out what this spirit is doing out here in the Mallow Fields.

It's clear he doesn't belong here. Judging by his clothes, I'd peg him as a native of the Anoka Desert. Either way, he's definitely dead. Yet, he doesn't realize he's no longer among the living. And again, I'm left holding the weight of the responsibility of telling him.

Why must I be the one to explain his demise? Him and how many others? How many times must I explain this sad fact to the lost souls I find here, wandering aimlessly and confused? The answer is: far too many times. But, alas, such is the job of a shepherd—someone who tends the flock of the dead.

He told me his name is Sinbad and I said my name is Bowie. Although we're still strangers to each other, I'm the only friend he has right now. Thus, I suppose, it's my job to get him where he needs to be, for whatever lies in store for him in the great beyond—something even I know nothing about. But, I will someday.

And, though it's a strange feeling to me now, after

11

all this time I've been doing what I do, I feel something for him—empathy? Perhaps. It's a feeling I haven't felt in a very long time. This job has a way of numbing you to the cold reality of death.

"I don't understand where I am or how I came to be here," he says as he faces me and shakes his head.

I wonder if he died in battle—he's really an incredible specimen of a man—tall and broad through the shoulders. He's muscular with a trim waist and long legs. He has the appearance of a warrior—someone trained to kill. Yet, there's something in his eyes that doesn't seem to follow that line of reasoning—something soft, kind.

"Let's reason this out," I say, starting slowly so I can gradually build my point. "How did you end up here?"

The handsome face starts to frown. "I'm unclear about that, actually. I was in the Caves of Larne with my companions." He looks at the ground of fluffy marshmallows that decorate the land of Sweetland. The path is graham cracker, the grass beyond candy glass of green and in the sky, clouds of various colored cotton candy.

I hate this place.

"I remember a fight..."

"And then?"

His eyes widen as he yells, "*Hassan!* Yes, Hassan sent me here." Seconds later, the conviction drains from his face and his brows furrow together in confusion. "No, that's not right."

12

"Well?" I gently ask. "Did Hassan send you here or didn't he?"

Ordinarily, I wouldn't bother with all these questions—instead, I'd lead him to the point where this world stops and the next starts and I would bid him adieu and send him on his way. But there's something about this stranger, about Sinbad, that begs more time.

He rubs his face hard. "No, I was trying to stop Hassan. He… he tried to take the Blue Faerie's wand for himself. And he came so close to having it!" He shakes his head. "Of course, I couldn't allow that. Hassan with the Blue Faerie's wand? It would have been disastrous!"

He's right. And although his story is quite alarming, I don't believe it's true. Those in death are notorious for confusing their dreams with what was their realities. Besides, everyone knows the Blue Faerie has been dead for a very long time, her wand lost with her. Yes, this poor, beautiful man is quite confused.

When the lost ones reach a crisis in their memories, the best thing to do is remain quiet until they work the truth of their situations out for themselves. Hence, I nod and allow him to continue.

"So, I picked the wand up and I… I pointed it at him…"

"And then?"

He nods as if to say he still remembers. "And I… I blasted him with it. Hassan disappeared then. May it be into oblivion."

"May it be so," I answer and then reach a hand

13

towards him, hoping we can start our short journey now that he's said whatever needs saying.

"And then... and then..." Horror contorts his face. "Something must have gone wrong! How else could I have ended up... all the way over here?" His face flushes in a way only the newly dead can manage. He looks at me with wide, concerned eyes. "Bowie, I must return with all haste!"

I watch Sinbad's body fade in and out from the strain of remembrance. It marks him as a lost soul in every sense of the word. He looks around anxiously, as if he seeks something to explain how he ended up in the Mallow Fields of Sweetland. Fortunately, I now understand what's happened to him, although he hasn't quite grasped it yet. Time to help him with that.

"You can't return, Sinbad," I say softly.

"In the name of all the gods and goddesses, why not?" he asks incredulously. "I need only to find my Roc and I'll be on my way." He looks up at the sky, searching for his gigantic bird but of course he won't see the Roc.

He shakes his head as he looks at me again. "I can't understand why my Roc hasn't come yet. I'm sensing we must be far from the caves, yes?"

I nod. "Yes, very far."

"But I've been wandering this field for such a long time already. Where could he be?"

I close my eyes for a second and try not to sigh. This is the part I really don't like—the part of this job that just leaves me cold.

14

He glances back at me. "Is this place enchanted or cursed? Is that why I can't leave?"

"No," I say, with another long and heartfelt sigh. "It's neither enchanted nor cursed."

"Then do you *know* what it is?"

"I do."

He clasps his hands in a supplicant manner. "Then please, tell me! I must return to the caves at once."

"Listen to me, Sinbad," I reply, viscerally dreading this next part. "I will try not to be indelicate, but I don't know how to say what you need to hear without... being direct."

"I must assume the news is unwelcome; but please continue?"

I nod. "You can't return to the caves and you can't leave the Mallow Fields because you're... dead."

To my utter surprise, he begins to laugh. He continues to laugh while I observe him quietly with a look of sheer exasperation. Mind you, Sinbad's response is slightly better than the usual threats and violence incited by such statements. But only slightly.

When he realizes my somber face remains unmoved, he finally ceases his laughter. "You think I'm dead?"

"Yes, because it's true."

"And what would that make you then?" he asks, still amused by the very suggestion that he's passed over.

"I'm a shepherdess," I answer and then wait for the truth to reach him.

15

He starts to laugh again, but then the smile falters on his lips. "A shepherdess?" he repeats, swallowing hard. "Are you kidding?"

"I wish I were." I shake my head and try to be understanding, try to imagine how I would feel were I in his place. "Sadly, you died in the caves," I explain. "I don't know the hows and whys of it, but I can only imagine such was your final resting place since it's the last place you remember."

"Yes, when I touched the Blue Faerie's wand," he fills in the rest and I just nod even though I still don't believe him.

"Your death... it simply hasn't registered with you yet."

He stares at me, examining my face for any sign of the lie he wishes it revealed. Then he looks at his fading hands and glances out over the field, understanding finally settling over his features. Now he knows why he's stuck here, materializing in and out, and why his Roc isn't coming for him. Now it begins to make sense to him.

I do feel compassion for Sinbad, even though I've dealt with this situation time and time again. But, where Sinbad is clearly upset by his predicament, not all who travel from the worlds of life to death are upset. Some are ready and they are the easiest to escort. Those who are prepared are usually joyful, eager even. The power to transcend the confines of their human bodies and the torment of crippling injuries, incurable diseases, or simple degeneration does that. But some are like

Sinbad, taken unexpectedly, and when they find themselves lost and alone, which they inevitably do, they must wait for someone like me to guide them to their destinies.

"Fuck," he says finally, his voice more subdued.

"I'm sorry," I say and reach for him, but he refuses to take my hand. It's then that I realize he's fully aware of who I am and what I'm meant to do.

"Then you're death?" he asks.

"No, I'm a shepherdess. I simply escort you to your next world, but I have nothing to do with the circumstances that brought you here."

He watches me and there's something suspicious in his eyes. "Is that why you're so beautiful?" he asks and takes me aback. I find it odd, but something within me swells at his words, swells over the fact that he finds me attractive. It's silly, really, because he and I are soon to part ways and I'll never see him again.

"You're beautiful to trick the unsuspecting into following you?" he continues.

"No, that's not why. I am… I look this way because I was simply… born looking this way."

"Then you're human? You aren't spirit?"

"Right," I nod. "But I have the ability to see through the veil—to see spirits and interact with them, hence how I'm able to take the role of your escort."

"If I died in the caves, why have I resurfaced here?"

"I honestly can't answer that," I reply on a shrug. It's a good question—there should have been a shepherd or shepherdess in the Anoka desert to welcome him to the other side. How he ended up here is anyone's guess. But it doesn't change the fact that there's only one place he's meant to go and I will lead him.

"Are you ready because it's time I escorted you to the Edge of Endless Night where your soul can be properly harvested. From there, you can choose whatever afterlife is currently available to—"

"By the nine hells, no!" he snaps at me viciously. "No, I'm not ready!"

I frown at him. "You have a perpetually blasphemous mouth."

"I'm a sailor! And I'm deceased! Do you expect me to offer prayers of thanks for such a short life?!"

I nod. "I suppose that's a fair reaction. Nevertheless, I have other duties I must attend to…" I gesture at him with my Shepherd's crook to let him know he isn't the only soul in need of direction. "Please come with me and I'll take you where you need to go."

He clears his throat and refuses to budge. "Am I allowed a request?"

I look at him. "What is your request?"

And his eyes start to roam down my body. "It has been a while since I knew a woman and before I travel to the next," he starts, but I immediately shake my head.

"If you're asking if I'll donate myself to your… beastly appetite, the answer is no."

He chuckles, and though I anger myself for

thinking it, I find him completely charming. "I thought it worth a try."

I glare at him. "Besides, you are spirit and I am human. It wouldn't work between us, anyway."

"Perhaps you should disrobe, and we can attempt it?"

"Perhaps not," I respond icily, but inside, something thrills at the idea. I've never been naked in front of a man before and while the thoughts have certainly crossed my mind on more than one occasion, I'm quite good at pushing them away.

He nods in defeat. "May I have one… other request granted?"

"Does it require anything sexual between the two of us?" I demand.

He chuckles again and I can't help but smile. Oh, but this man is a dangerous one.

"No," he answers. Then he takes a deep breath. "I wish for my soul to be reaped at my home in the Anoka Desert."

"I'm sorry, Sinbad, but I can only take you to the Edge of Endless Night. I'm not allowed to take you anywhere else."

"It is my last dying wish," he insists, as I think better of telling him it isn't his last dying wish because he's already died. "Please, Bowie," he insists, eyes going wide as he shakes his head. He really is a handsome man. It's a shame he met his end so early. "You must understand," he continues, "I only wish to check on my companions and my clan; I must make

19

certain they're all right. Perhaps I can be of some help to them, despite my… current condition."

I don't reply, but I shake my head no.

"How can so lovely a woman as yourself have such a cold heart?" he scoffs as he glares at me. "It's as if you're made of stone."

"How can a seasoned sailor of the ocean fail to see what's right in front of him?" I counter. "Your life is over—all that awaits you now is the afterlife."

He crosses his arms and glowers at me. "I refuse to go anywhere until you agree to my terms."

I shrug. "Well, that's your choice, and I respect it." I look back at the souls that start to appear in the Mallow Fields—souls that require my services. I look back at Sinbad and shake my head. "I have to go now— I've already spent too much time with you. I will return on the morrow."

He stands stubbornly to one side, allowing me to pass and attend to my business. I restrain a sigh, but blow a frustrated breath out of my nose. That didn't go the way it was supposed to. I was supposed to simply hand him off to the afterlife, just as I've done with so many souls before him. I wasn't supposed to get trapped in conversation and I definitely wasn't supposed to notice his physical attributes. Clearly, I wasn't heavy-handed enough with him, which is why he's still lost in the Mallow Fields. I've failed.

Better luck tomorrow, I suppose. Of course, I know what will happen next. Sinbad, like all the others, will try to leave the Mallow Fields, but he can't. The only way he could leave is if his soul tethers itself to me, but the chances of that happening are next to nothing. He won't even realize that's an option and, of course, I won't mention it.

No, he'll be right where I left him when I come back tomorrow. And eventually he'll stop resisting the inevitable—no one wanders for very long in the limbo between life and death. Eventually, they all beg to leave this place because they get tired of being trapped here with nowhere else to go.

It'd be much easier for me if I could insist that Sinbad depart at once and stop wasting my time. But I can't. He must accompany me, yes, but he's allowed one final option at the end of his life and that option is the choice *when* he departs this place.

I promise myself that tomorrow I'll be sterner with him—I'll take him to the Edge and I'll insist he continue forward and then I'll be free of Sinbad and I'll never have to see him again.

Chapter Two
Bowie

The following day, I return to the Mallow Fields and, of course, I find Sinbad right where I left him. I ask if he's willing to come with me and he launches into a long-winded story about saving a king's horse from a magical seahorse.

And much though I hate to admit it, I find myself enraptured by his story and by the way he tells it—with so much feeling, so much color in his words and expressions. It's almost as if he's opened a storybook and began reading to me. Before I know it, a whole afternoon has disappeared. And that's when I realize I'm falling under the same spell I did yesterday—there's something about this man that's causing me to fail in my duties.

I can't waste any more valuable time on him—not when there are so many other souls who require the assistance of a shepherd—so many other souls who need to understand why they've arrived here and where they're to go next.

Yet, I find I can't stop Sinbad from continuing his tales—this one about a time when he defeated four

22

men. When he finally ends his tale, he informs me that he's still not ready to embark on his final journey and, exasperated, I must be on my way again.

The next day plays out similarly. And the day after that.

Each day, when I return to escort Sinbad to the beyond, he tells me a new adventure from the days when he was still alive. And even though I grow increasingly frustrated with myself, I find I look forward to his stories and when I'm standing before him, I'm eager to play the part of riveted audience.

You don't want him to leave, I tell myself. *And that's dangerous because it's your job to ensure he does leave. And what if he tethers himself to you?*

The chances of that happening are next to nothing.

As I watch his eyes light up and that charming smile turn up the ends of his lips, I find myself enthralled yet again. Of course, I expect some of his stories are based on truth and others mere fancies (most I'm quite sure are exaggerations). Being a sailor, I don't doubt that he must have seen some interesting phenomena, but the number of stories he has begs the question as to how it would be possible for one man to experience as many things as he has in one lifetime.

As engaging as these stories can be, though, the fact remains that Sinbad is merely languishing in limbo needlessly. That and I'm failing to do my job—mainly because he's making it more difficult than it needs to be.

On the eighth day, Sinbad prepares to begin

another long tale, but I no longer have the patience left to hear it. I've fought with myself so many times now that I realize Sinbad's time is up. I have to insist he move to his next adventure.

"No more!" I tell him, shaking my head. "We can't tarry any longer, Sinbad," I explain. "There are other lost souls who must be guided from this field, and I can't do that while paying attention to all your wild stories."

He seems offended by my outburst and… hurt. "I thought you liked listening to them."

"I merely indulged you as a courtesy," I lie, figuring it's now time for me to be heavy-handed and strict with him. If I give him the figurative inch, he'll take the mile. And though I did and do love his stories, he has to go. He can't stay here. And I can't become more attached to him than I already am.

"Indulged me?" he repeats, glaring at me.

"Yes," I answer as I remind myself I've tried to be understanding with him and lenient, but I have a job to do and he's keeping me from doing it. "The time has come for you to move on with all the other souls."

"Must I depart so soon?" he asks, sounding deflated.

"Do you want to stay in these fields forever?" I can't imagine he would.

He looks around with a pensive gaze. "No, but I also don't want to leave… I'm just… I'm not ready."

"That's what everyone says, Sinbad. No one is ever ready for his life to end."

24

He looks at me and there's something burning in his eyes, something rebellious. "There must be another way?"

"Another way for what?"

"To avoid the path before me. Another way to remain here."

There is, but I won't tell him what that way is. Souls aren't supposed to tether themselves to me. They're supposed to move on. I shake my head as I begin to understand. He likes to recount his many stories because he knows he'll never see such sights again—he'll never experience the incredible situations he has thus far, and he wants more of them.

"There is no other course, Sinbad, and I'm sorry for that," I say kindlier this time. "This is just the way it is. Even a harvester of souls like myself must face that inevitable moment someday."

"Very well," he says. "I shall vex you no longer, Shepherdess. I'm ready to go."

Finally, I think with a little exasperation, even as my heart drops down to my toes at the thought that I'll never see him again. I don't know how it's possible but in the last eight days, I've thought of little else other than Sinbad and his wild stories. I will miss him—that much is certain.

"Let's be on our way, then. If you'll follow me?"

He waves me ahead and gives me a half-bow. "Lead on, beautiful lady."

We begin to walk across the fields. At first, we're both silent and I regret being so firm with him, but then

I remind myself it had to be done. This is the only way—Sinbad no longer belongs here. His life is over. Destiny decided that, and there must be a reason why.

After a short while, he clears his throat and asks, "Would you mind if I told you another story?" He pauses a moment. "I find talking keeps my mind off the immediate... future."

I give my consent. I must admit, the famous sailor continues to grow on me. His bravado and stubbornness aside, he's excessively handsome, funny, and charming. And he's an expert storyteller. I can't recall the last time I was so amused.

So, I listen to his next tale as we make our trek. This adventure involves tricking the old man of the sea. Sinbad was enslaved by this man until he plied the codger with wine and made his escape. Once again, I have to wonder how much of the story is strictly facts and how much was born from his imagination.

Finally, we arrive at the border of life and death, the hazy spot between dire oblivion and enthusiastic vibrancy. Sinbad shudders when we enter, but I know he has nothing to fear.

Turning around, I recite my oft-practiced farewell speech. "This is where we part our ways, Sinbad. You need only take one step across this border and you'll join the afterlife."

Sinbad swallows visibly. "You know, now that we're here, I'm uncertain if I want to join the afterlife."

"Sinbad..." I warn him.

"Please, Bowie, you've granted me this much time.

May I have just a few moments longer?"

I've been a shepherdess for far too long not to recognize a stall tactic when I hear one. Yet, I allow him the time, even as I know I will. I've already made so many allowances for Sinbad that I've never made for anyone else. I really will miss him.

After he tells me another story, something heavy appears in his eyes. "Then I suppose it's time?" he asks.

I nod.

"You can't stay with me here a bit longer?"

I shake my head.

"Why?" he asks.

"Because I'm the only shepherdess in the Mallow Fields," I explain. "My job is gathering souls like yours and escorting them here."

"And you can't tarry any longer?" There's a hopeful expression in his eyes. "I know you enjoy our conversations more than you let on." He looks at me and forces a smile to my lips.

"And why would you think that?"

He chuckles. "Because I captivate your attention and when my tales become scary or intense, your lovely blue eyes widen, just like a child's." He grows quiet then and reaches out to take my hand. "Tell me, Bowie, has our time together meant as much to you as it has to me?"

I take a deep breath and realize I can't answer his question because if I do, he'll come up with some other way to beg my time. So, I shake my head. "Truth is, I've already taken way too much time with you,

27

Sinbad. No complaints—and I'll always treasure your stories—but many lost souls are waiting for me to return."

"Is there no one else to escort them?" he asks.

"No," I reply with a note of despair. "The other shepherds who helped with my duties have all been killed," I answer in a softer tone, shaking my head. "Just as so many shepherds have been recently."

Sinbad narrows his eyes. "Why are so many shepherds dying?"

"Morningstar's edict," I reply bitterly. "He ordered all of us to be executed."

"Executed?" he responds, shocked. "For what reason?"

"I wish I knew," I tell him, shaking my head as I shrug. "I'm sure it fits into Morningstar's diabolical plan somehow. I just don't know how exactly." The weight of my knowledge suddenly crashes on me like a pile of rocks. That's another reason why I must keep guiding souls to the afterlife, because if I don't, who will?

Sinbad takes a slow breath. "Is it safe for you to return to your post?"

I tilt my head to the side as I consider his question. "Probably not, but it doesn't change the fact that these souls need to be guided."

"Yet you risk losing your own life?"

"I suppose so," I answer quickly as I take a deep breath. I don't like thinking about or discussing this subject.

"Bowie, do you mind leaving me here and allowing me to cross over when I'm ready to do so?" Sinbad asks, pausing a moment before adding. "I understand why you need to return."

I put a hand on his shoulder as I think to myself, I'll give him this last request. "Don't wait too long, Sinbad," I say in a soft voice. "Lingering here only makes it… harder the longer you stay. A better place awaits you elsewhere." I look over the border wistfully. "A place far away from here."

He puts his hand on mine and something passes through us then—a feeling of energy from his hand to mine. It almost feels like thousands of ants marching along my skin.

"Thank you for your kindness, Bowie. And for listening to my stories. I will never forget you."

"I have to go," I reply, and though I don't mean to sound terse, I can't help it. I want to say more, but for some strange reason, I start to choke up. I have to turn away before I lose control and tears bleed from my eyes. It's an odd reaction and one I've never had before—I've done this job a long time and the first thing you learn to lose is your sadness for the plight of those you deliver. You become numb after a while—it's just something that happens.

So, why haven't you been numb to Sinbad? Why did you allow him to take the time he needs and allow him to distract you with all his stories? Why is he different?

I don't have an answer for myself.

29

As I walk away hastily, I fear I've grown too attached. I rarely spend time getting to know any members of my flock. And now that we're parted, I feel as if I'm… strangely going to miss him and his seemingly unending stories. I glance down at my hand and rub it because the feeling of energy still hums along my skin.

###

On my way back into town, I spot a group of men and women gathered in the square. Even though I know I shouldn't waste any more precious time, especially when my duty is to the Mallow Fields, I move in to take a closer look. It's almost as if I can't stop myself.

Toward the front of the group, I notice three extremely attractive men. One of them is holding a dark stone in his hand—I'm fairly sure it's a soul stone. As I approach, the stone begins to glow a deep, dark crimson. Several of the onlookers gasp as the men walk past them. All eyes are fastened on the stone and I notice the three men look around, as if searching for the reason the stone has started to glow red.

When they approach me, the soul stone changes into an even deeper color, growing brighter until it becomes a shocking red that reflects the light in all directions. I'm almost blinded by the brilliant light.

The three men look at each other before the one holding the stone speaks directly to me.

"Hello, lass."

"Hello," I answer.

"Allow me to introduce myself: I am Dolion Winters."

Dolion Winters is tall—almost as tall as Sinbad. I would guess him to be six-foot-two or so. He wears his brown hair long, tied back in a knot at his neck and his green eyes gleam with something that looks like mischief. His beard is short and tidy and I have the feeling his bed is never lacking female company.

I find it odd he's bothering to introduce himself to me—as if I'm anyone of importance. "Pleased to meet you," I answer, before attempting to proceed on my way. The guilt of being gone so long is now really taking a toll on me and, strangely, the pack beneath my arm and my shepherd's crook seem somehow weightier than they were this morning. I'm sure that weightiness has everything to do with the sadness that descended on me the moment I parted ways with Sinbad.

But Dolion's voice stops me. "And your name?"

"Bowie," I reply, holding up my hand, with my shepherd's pack, to shield my eyes from the stone's intense light.

"Well, Ms. Bowie," he continues, lowering the stone as he stares at me with wide eyes. "The glowing of the soul stone officially verifies you're a Chosen One!"

Chapter Three
Bowie

After a full minute of eyeing Dolion Winters skeptically, I manage to say, "I'm a... what?"

"A Chosen One," he repeats as if it were as obvious as the crook in my hand. "Surely you've heard of those special few selected by Destiny, herself, to prevail in the decisive battle against Morningstar."

I just look at him blankly for a moment as I try to fully comprehend his words. Me? A Chosen One? Has he lost his mind?

"Everyone knows about the Chosen, yes, but I can't be one of them!" I say, eyeing him as if he's in leave of his sense, which he very well must be if he believes I'm one of the Chosen. "I'm a lowly Shepherdess from the Mallow Fields!" Chosen? Hardly!

Dolion Winters holds up the stone again, nearly blinding me in the process. "Do you not see the brilliance in the light coming from this stone?"

"I do," I answer.

"And you realize what this stone is?"

I nod. "Yes—it's a soul stone."

32

"Right. Thus, the stone does not lie."

I look around myself, as if trying to find another person among us who could be responsible for setting the stone ablaze. But there's no one standing close enough to it. As Dolion watches me, he takes a few steps closer and holds the stone out toward me and, in response, the stone glows even more brightly.

Yes, it's certainly responding to me, but how or why, I have no idea. All I do know is I simply can't be a Chosen One.

Yet, Dolion is correct—the stone can't lie.

As inclined as I am to deny it, I know what he says must be true. Yet, perhaps the stone has made a mistake? But, how could that be? The stone can't make mistakes. The legends of these soul stones are public knowledge and have been for some time. As the legends go, when in close proximity to a Chosen One, each stone will glow red with the blood of Morningstar. I've even glimpsed some of them in my travels. Yet this marks the first time one has ever glowed in my presence.

As if my life weren't complicated enough...

Dolion interrupts my thoughts by suddenly grabbing my arm. "Now that we have found you, you must come with us."

"What?" I exclaim, alternately glaring at him and the hand that holds me. "Go with you? No, I most certainly won't!"

Who the hell does he think he is?

"Our orders are explicit, Ms. Bowie," he explains,

lips tight. I can tell by his expression that he's not someone who is used to others arguing with him. "We were told to escort you to the front lines once we found you and took you into our custody."

"Front lines? Of what?" I screech, vainly trying to pull my arm free. "I don't even know who you are!"

"I've introduced myself," Dolion says, frowning impatiently.

"Regardless, I don't know you from Adam," I continue, still glaring at him. "And I'm not going anywhere with you."

"It is Destiny," he insists. "You are the reason we've come here with the stone—you are the person we were sent to find."

"I can't explain why or how the stone has pointed towards me as being… Chosen, but it's wrong," I insist.

"It's not wrong," Dolion says, anger marring his features. "And you are Chosen, which means you have a destiny to fulfill."

"And how would you know what my destiny is?" I demand. "Like I said, you don't even know me!"

"I will explain everything later."

"No, you tell me now!" I insist, all the while my responsibilities in the Mallow Fields continue to beat upon the back door of my mind.

"Look," he says, pulling up his shirt and revealing a distinctive tattoo. His two companions follow suit, displaying the same tattoo on their chests. I know the mark immediately, before he explains it.

"Apparently, these gentlemen are members of the Guild," a familiar voice says from behind me. I whirl around and find, much to my shock and, okay, pleasure, Sinbad standing there, although he's now mostly transparent—just like the ghost he is. But it should be impossible for him to be here—he was never supposed to be able to leave the Mallow Fields!

Unless…

"What are you doing here?" I ask indignantly, angry with him for betraying me. "You promised to stay by the threshold until you were ready to cross over."

"No, no," Sinbad replies, shaking his head as he holds up his arms as if to say he's innocent. "I said I'd cross over *when* I was ready. What I did in the meantime was never specified." His smile broadens. "And you said I wouldn't be able to leave the Mallow Fields… looks like you were wrong."

I take a deep breath and reach out to touch him. As soon as I do, I feel the same energy pulse from his skin and into my hand. Yes, it's as I feared—he's tethered himself to me. This is the only time a spirit has ever tethered themselves to me and I don't know much about it, other than the fact that I had to make myself open to Sinbad, in order for him to tether himself. Thus, this is as much my fault as it is his. Blast!

"Sinbad, I trusted you," I start, but Dolion Winters interrupts me.

"You're a ghost?" he asks Sinbad with a puzzled expression and his companions do the same.

35

Apparently, they've never seen one before. Sometimes I forget that most folk can't see or interact with spirits. Because it's part of my job description, I suppose I take it for granted.

Sinbad regards him with little interest. "I am, and I'm currently trying to understand why you're trying to convince Bowie to accompany you."

"Are you her protector?" Dolion asks.

Sinbad clears his throat and looks at me for a split second before turning back to Dolion. "I am. And who are you?"

"We are the sworn protectors of the Chosen Ones," Dolion answers. "And perhaps it might come to you as a surprise, but Bowie is one of the Chosen."

"Is she?" Sinbad asks, looking at me with amusement. I can't say why, but his expression causes butterflies to alight in my stomach.

"Because we are the protectors of the Chosen, Ms. Bowie must come with us at once."

"I am a shepherd and I can't leave my post. Not when there are countless souls I need to lead to the other side," I protest, motioning toward Sinbad with my free hand. "Case in point!" I glare at him and he simply smiles back at me as if he had no hand to play in the fact that he's standing right there before me. "Sinbad still needs to cross over."

"My dear," Sinbad starts, but I interrupt him.

"Of course, if he'd done so when he was supposed to…"

"I wish to accompany you," Sinbad says simply as

my mouth drops open in outrage.

"Accompany me?" I repeat, shaking my head. "You will do no such thing and I... the only place I'm going is back to my post at the Mallow Fields!"

One of the men shrugs. "I don't see any reason why Sinbad can't come along with us." He smiles at me. "He's obviously tethered himself to you."

"Tethered?" Sinbad repeats as he looks at me.

"Ugh," I respond and then nod, figuring the truth is out so there's no reason to deny it now.

"What is tethering, Bowie?" Sinbad pushes.

I face him. "It's when your spirit tethers itself to me and therefore, you can leave the Mallow Fields. Not only that, but both of us have a connection now whereby we'll be able to feel each other and always know where the other is located."

"Well, lucky me," Sinbad says with a wide grin.

"Regardless, I still need to escort you back to the Mallow Fields!" I declare, before turning to face the three men in front of me. "Sinbad has somewhere else he's supposed to be, and it's my job to take him there!"

"A place that will no doubt still be there when our task is complete," Sinbad replies, smiling broadly. "In the meantime, I'd be honored to accompany my faithful, ever patient shepherdess in her quest as a Chosen One." He clears his throat. "Besides, as her personal protector, I deem it my job."

Then he looks at me, and his grin is broad and victorious. He's probably aware that the last thing I want to do is travel with three men unchaperoned—

three strangers. At least I know Sinbad—well, I know him better than I know them.

Wait, I tell myself. *What are you thinking? Are you actually considering going with them? Men you don't even know?*

Well, if I'm really a Chosen One, what choice do I have? I argue back.

I can't decide who upsets me more, the man gripping my arm or the disobedient spirit who refuses to end his mortal journey.

"By what name are you called, spirit?" Dolion asks.

Sinbad's grin broadens. "The same name I took in life, I am Sinbad."

"Very well, Mr. Sinbad, you may join us," he says, waving Sinbad off dismissively. It's obvious he thinks we've wasted enough of his time already. Well, blight to him and blight to the rest of them!

"Wait," I say as he drags me after him. "I haven't agreed to go anywhere with you!"

"That is of little importance," Dolion says. "We are now your protectors and we are responsible for delivering you to the other Chosen." Then he stops and turns to look at me. "Trained first, of course." He starts walking forward again. "Our horses are just tied up behind the tavern and we have an extra for you."

Trained? What in the blazes is he talking about? "But!" I yell out, shaking my head. "What of my post? What of my job?"

"What of it?" Dolion asks.

"I have responsibilities!"

"And none of those responsibilities are as important as your responsibility to the Chosen."

I dig my heels in a little harder and argue, "I'm not prepared for any clash against Morningstar."

"Which is why we plan to train you in the mastery of combat," he calmly replies.

Twisting his thumb, I manage to pull free of his grasp. Then I take two steps before the Guild companions freeze me in place with their drawn weapons. No one comes to my defense. Sinbad just looks at me and shakes his head as if to say there's nothing he can do and he's quite right. The most he can do is leave a bit of ectoplasm on them. Blast!

"Understand this, Bowie," Dolion says from behind me, "if you refuse to let us help you, you shall be ill-equipped when the time comes." He puts his sword away and then lays a pair of gentle hands on my shoulders.

"You are forcing me to accompany you against my will!"

He nods. "I understand how you feel. No one *wants* to battle Morningstar. No one can blame you for admitting your fear. But I can assure you of this: sooner or later, this fight will happen. When Morningstar comes for you, and he will, you'll need the training we offer you now to defeat him."

"That sounds like a death sentence," I retort. "And will I just reap myself when he finishes me off?"

"Surely you mean *if* he finishes you off, not *when*,"

39

Sinbad interjects.

"Not helping," I growl at him.

"If you accept our assistance," Dolion says, "that tragic event won't happen."

I try one last gambit. "And how do I know you are whom you say you are? Those tattoos could easily be faked."

"They can't be faked, Bowie," Sinbad contradicts me, even as I realize the truth for myself. "Once you've seen enough of them, you know every detail by heart." But, with the way Sinbad studies Dolion, I can't say the spirit trusts him. In fact, I think it might be safe to say he doesn't.

"Do you have any reason to distrust the Guild?" Dolion asks me.

"No," I reply honestly. "The Guild has never given me any cause to distrust them—I've only ever known them to be noble and altruistic."

"Then I think we've wasted enough valuable time," Dolion says. "Will you please come with us?" I can tell he asks the question just to make me feel better, but I really have no say in the subject. In fact, I'm fairly sure if I refused and ran off, they'd simply hunt me down and force me to travel with them.

With an audible sigh, I nod, figuring I have little choice otherwise. As to my post? I don't know—I suppose whatever shall happen is in the process of happening.

The trio guide us to their horses.

I pair up with Dolion while Sinbad floats beside us.

40

Seeing the expression on his face, I can only assume he's thrilled at his newfound ability to ride the air around us. And I'm sure he's even more thrilled to have dodged his duty of passing into the next realm by being tethered to me. Although he's barely visible now, I can still see a smile on his face. Traveling abreast, his animated voice relates his own encounters with the Guild.

"You would think you would be out of stories by this point," I grumble.

Dolion squints at our ghostly companion, before turning to face me. "Is he still there? You can still hear him?"

"Yes. You can't?"

"It's nearly impossible for me to see him, much less, hear him." He shakes his head. "I had figured the spirit had remained behind."

"Wishful thinking," Sinbad answers, frowning at Dolion. It almost seems as if Sinbad's… jealous of him?

"Oh, really," I reply casually. I've been shepherding the deceased for so long, I sometimes forget I'm one of the few who can hear and see them clearly at all times. The more freshly dead they are, the easier it is for the living to see them. "You could see him quite clearly earlier?"

"I wouldn't describe him as clear," Dolion responds. "He was more a whitish mass."

"But you could hear him?"

Dolion nods. "That I could."

41

###

When we are far outside city limits and riding with nothing but forest on either side, the sun dips below the horizon, and my riding companion announces, "We'll stop here for the night."

I look around at the darkness enveloping us. "Here?" I ask skeptically. There's nothing but miles and miles of trees and the moonlight showing between their skeletal branches.

"I promise you're in very safe hands, Bowie," Dolion assures me as he dismounts. "Once we build a hot fire and have a bite to eat, things will seem much more hospitable." He clears his throat. "And I can promise you... we are all gentlemen."

"As well you should be," Sinbad says as he glares at Dolion. "I wouldn't allow you to lay a hand on her."

I give Sinbad a smile of thanks and he simply nods at me, but keeps his eyes on Dolion. As far as I can tell, Dolion still can't see or hear him. Odd.

I get off the horse warily. "And where am I to sleep?"

One of the men holds up a rolled-up bundle for my viewing. "We packed an extra tent to ensure your uninterrupted privacy."

"Very thoughtful of you," I reply, although I'm not thrilled about the idea of sleeping in a tent, alone or otherwise. Actually, I'm not thrilled with the prospect of being here at all. And if I'm ever able to return to the

Mallow Fields, I don't know how I'll explain my disappearance. It's not as though a person gets called to become one of the Chosen every day. In fact, the more I think about it, the more improbable and completely ridiculous it seems. Yet, the soul stone glowed red, just as the legends said it would.

Sinbad looks around suspiciously, indicating he shares my lack of enthusiasm with the situation. "I don't like this."

Without any reply, I take the tent proffered by the Guildsman. If nothing else, I shall be the one to decide where I sleep tonight.

Chapter Four
Bowie

Once the men finish setting up camp, they quickly build a fire.

Then they cook two whole chickens and some ears of corn they purchased before we left, turning them on a spit above the flames. When I'm not watching the food, my eyes are fastened on the Guildsmen. I'm still uncomfortable around them and I don't even know the names of the other two men.

As we enjoy our cooked chicken and corn, along with fat steins filled with deep brown ale, my mood lightens a little. Yes, I'm still mad at the way these strangers dragged me along with them, virtually against my will, but the satisfying combination of food and ale bolsters me enough to ask about the identities of my other two companions.

"Ah, that is an oversight on our part, isn't it?" Dolion politely admits. He gestures with his mug to his nearest companion.

"I am Claude Frollo of Wonderland," the man says. He's shorter than Dolion and stouter, not quite as handsome but still very attractive. His hair has a strawberry cast and his eyes are the color of honey. "A holy man or at least, such is what I once was. I used to be a member of the Church of the Seven Joys, but now I'm trying to make amends."

I smile at him. "Stepping away from any spiritual path can't be an easy undertaking."

"True, but my life changed significantly after I saved another of the Chosen Ones. She is a lovely lass by the name of Rose."

Dolion gives him a mock toast. "A worthy endeavor must always have a compelling reason." Before I can ask what he means by that, he motions to the remaining man.

"Jack Cuore is the name I received at birth," this man says as his introduction. This man is immense—towering over all the others and with his somewhat unkempt hair, he appears to be quite the barbarian. His beard is long and his eyes have that same feral quality as his voice. "I was born in Wonderland. But for better or worse, I was exiled."

"I'm sorry," I start to say, but he interrupts me as he shakes his head.

"I'm not." He continues to nod. "I'm also a mage." An afterthought seems to occur to him then. "Speaking of which, I'll be your tutor in the subject of magic."

"Magic?" I repeat doubtfully.

"I'm a patient teacher."

"You'll need a lot more than patience if you think someone like me can be trained to go up against Morningstar," I say, my mood souring at the dismal reminder of why we're all here.

For his part, Jack Cuore doesn't seem offended. "You're unskilled now, but you possess more power than you realize, Bowie."

I take a bitter swig of the ale. "Well, it certainly doesn't seem that way."

"That'll change as soon as we begin your training."

"And when shall I expect my training to begin?" All of this—meeting Sinbad, coming across the Guild members, learning I'm a Chosen One—it's all happened so fast, I can scarcely believe it. And as I discuss my upcoming training, I'm almost in shock as I do so.

"Oh, soon. Very soon." He nods toward their undeclared leader. "As Dolion so often reminds everyone, we have very little time. Therefore, we must do whatever we can as we travel."

"And where is it that we're traveling to?" I ask.

"The battlefield," Dolion replies.

I frown at him. "We're traveling directly into battle?"

"The battle rages, therefore we must bring you to it," he answers.

"Lovely," I say with a sneer, tearing into the flesh of my half of the chicken. Our conversation almost kills my appetite, but I know I must eat while I can.

"You'll be fine," Dolion says with a nod, picking up an ear of corn. "In fact, I'm certain you'll exceed all of our expectations."

"You'll excuse me if I confess my doubts about

46

that."

"Who doesn't have doubts in the beginning?" Sinbad chirps in the background.

"I'm sure you do," Dolion says to me. "But everything you need will soon come to you. You were meant to do this, Bowie."

I gesture with my chicken leg at Jack Cuore. "So, he's my magic teacher…" I indicate Claude Frollo. "And he's my spiritual support…" I gesture at Dolion and ask, "what part do you play in all of this?"

"I'm your Commander-at-Arms," he replies. "I will take you into battle and ensure your success."

"And what exactly does that entail?"

"I'll do everything within my power to protect you, including sacrificing my own life, if necessary."

Sinbad's subsequent scoff and choice remark make me chuckle. When the other three men look at me in confusion, I shake my head and answer their unspoken question. "Sorry, Sinbad was just saying that sacrificing one's life for a Chosen One is vastly overrated, in his experience."

"Ah, I suppose so from his perspective," Dolion says, squinting into the darkness as if trying to see Sinbad for himself. "Interesting. Then your friend acknowledges having been around at least one Chosen One himself?"

I don't know that I'd call Sinbad my 'friend' but I don't correct Dolion. Instead, I look back and see Sinbad, who's barely visible in the darkness behind me. None of the others can see him any longer. I'm just glad they could see him earlier, lest they believe I'm completely mad.

"Just between us, dear Bowie," Sinbad says, "I care very little for these men or their intentions. Guild or no Guild. We know far too little about them." Naturally, I agree with Sinbad, but I have the presence of mind not to acknowledge his comment.

Oblivious to my ghostly companion's words, Dolion continues his spiel. "Morningstar's army will be ready for war soon. They are gathering in great numbers and setting up camps. So, your first task is to wipe out each camp—or at least as many of the people in those camps that you can—to keep Morningstar's troops away from the ultimate battle. Otherwise, their massive numbers will overrun us."

"Won't Morningstar's mere presence make their numbers irrelevant, anyway?" I ask.

"Only if no Chosen Ones confront him," Claude replies. "The Chosen Ones need to focus on Morningstar, himself, rather than his forces."

"Which is why we need to eliminate as many of his forces as soon as possible," Dolion concurs.

"What do you mean by 'eliminate' exactly?" I ask innocently enough.

The three men look at each other with the same doubt that's been plaguing me since they dragged me along with them.

"Why, exterminating them, of course," Jack says.

"I think you're all confused about me and what sort of person I am," I reply on a shrug, hoping this conversation will be enough for them to send me back on my merry way. "My job and purpose in this life is to shepherd the newly deceased to the afterlife. I'm not prepared or trained to kill anyone." Well, anyone vibrant and alive, anyway. I have helped those who are on their way out of this life—using the implements from my shepherd's pack. But I've never cut a person down who was in the blossom of his life.

"That, Bowie, was your old life," Dolion explains slowly. "You're now a Chosen One, which means you have a new purpose and task."

"A new task that involves killing people!" I say to him, outrage at the idea growing as I glare at him.

"Either Morningstar prevails or we prevail," he answers on a shrug. "Death is inevitable. You, of all people, must know that."

"I understand that, but I don't know how I feel about being the person responsible for delivering all that death."

"What would you have us do, then?" Dolion asks. "Try to talk to them?" Then he chuckles as if the idea is idiotic. I understand that war is bloody and death is certain, but that doesn't mean I want any part of it. I tell them as much and then it's so quiet, only the sounds of the crackling fire and the insects humming from the wilderness around us can be heard.

"Bowie, are you all right?" Dolion asks.

"Certainly not!" I bark at him.

"I know it's a lot to take in. What can we do to make it easier for you to accept?"

"I don't know," I answer as I push to my feet and decide I've had enough for one evening—I've been forced into this whole situation and I'm not happy about it. "I... I want to be alone," I explain as I then stomp off towards the tent they've set up for me.

"You just need more time to get used to the idea," Dolion calls after me. "We'll talk about it in the morning." His nonchalant apathy makes me even more furious and I have half a mind to leave this place now. But being out in the middle of nowhere, there's nothing I can do tonight and, besides, I have no idea where I am and no idea how to get back to the Mallow Fields.

No sooner do I throw myself under the covers than I start crying into my pillow because I realize how desperate my situation is. I can't run from what I am—from what the soul stone said I was. I'm a Chosen One and that means I can't escape my calling. Destiny brought me here and that means I need to suck it up and do my part.

No matter how unprepared I am.

The truth is: I'm torn. Being a Chosen One is very important, and it should be considered a huge honor. Not only an honor, but also a privilege. I'm obliged to do my part to stop Morningstar. But how can I? Killing people, no matter which side they're on—it's the complete antithesis of my life as a shepherd—as someone who leads the dead to the next level of existence. Furthermore, I'm not a violent person, so how in the world am I meant to wipe out whole camps of people? I sob into my pillow until I fall asleep.

50

Sinbad, to his credit, remains silent.

Before drifting off, my last thought is: how do I reap souls who aren't ready to go? Men like Sinbad who still have life they're eager to live? How can I take responsibility for ending their lives myself? The image of slaughtered bodies on a battlefield evokes unparalleled terror and grief in me. I've seen it on the faces of far too many of my flock over the years.

Then leave, Bowie, I tell myself. *If you don't believe this is your destiny, then leave.*

Chapter Five
Claude

A sound outside my tent awakens me in the dead of night.

Actually, that is untrue. I had already been awakened from the nightmares which plague me each and every night. Nightmares that only seem to have started since I teamed up with Dolion and Jack.

When I get up to see what it is, I catch a glimpse of Bowie making her way through the woods nearby. By the time I follow her, she's already in the clearing on the other side. Seeing her gives me a sense of ominous foreboding and I do hope she doesn't decide to really make good on an escape—not in the middle of the forest. Surely, she would have no idea where to go or how to get there. She carries with her the small pack she had earlier and the shepherd's crook—something I never see her without.

I watch her sort out the various tools she pulls from her pack, laying them out neatly on a broad, wooden stump. She hangs her lantern on a nearby branch to illuminate her makeshift worktable. Hmm, then she isn't attempting an escape? Then what is she doing?

I stay back and observe her as she carefully arranges extra glass panes for her lantern, fluids, pieces of cloth, some vials of poison and a number of implements meant to deliver a merciful death—salves, potions, bloodletting stems. Anyone who heard her speech earlier—Dolion comes to mind—would be surprised to see those last items. I, however, know better. Her reluctance to kill anyone isn't because she hasn't done so before. Rather, it's because she's never killed anyone who wasn't poised on the verge of death, in need of a nudge to take the final step across the threshold. There are times when shepherds are called in to ease the demise of the person dying—such is viewed as a more empathetic approach to easing the transference to the beyond.

To some people—again, Dolion comes to mind—there is little difference in putting someone out of their earthly misery and killing a healthy enemy right where they stand. But for someone like Bowie, there is a great deal of difference. Putting someone out of their earthly misery is motivated by kindness and mercy. Ending a tortured life with dignity and grace to free a captive soul from its confinement on the mortal plane is a favor. The other killing is the intentional taking of life from someone who wishes to live, possibly with a family they love or deeds left unfinished. Such souls aren't ready to be freed from their current life and will thus be tormented forever in the beyond. If they even move to the beyond…

So, even if a person is deemed evil, someone of

Bowie's bent will look beyond that. And while I understand Bowie's misgivings and her doubt, such luxuries are impossible to afford in times of war. The enemy has their orders and we have ours. We each have a mutual duty to destroy the enemy in the name of our Commander-in-Chief. While I respect Bowie's feelings on the matter, she must understand *this* war is different. It is literally good versus evil, and there will be men, women and children casualties for both side—the innocents aren't spared from indiscriminate war machines. It is unfortunate, yes, but it is true. If the enemy prevails, however, the loss of innocent life will be a given—as will the take-over of Fantasia by those with malicious intent. If that comes to pass, the rest of us will be doomed.

Bowie glances up, looking directly at me, and holds my gaze. How long did she know I was standing here? I can see tears reflected in her eyes before she quickly looks away again, talking to someone in front of her I can't see. I'm certain it must be the spirit, Sinbad, who appears to be some form of companion to the shepherdess.

Whether he's a threat to any of us remains unclear. Obviously, there isn't much he can do in his present incorporeal state. But he does have her ear, which presents its own dangers to our mission. Then again, I may be overly harsh in my judgment. He could just be a lost soul who desperately needs her guidance to move on. If the three of us permanently interrupted that, I'm truly sorry for him. No one deserves to linger in such an unnatural state. Yet, for now, it can't be helped.

"Forgive my intrusion," I tell her. "I didn't mean to pry."

"It's fine," she says with a shrug, her voice sounding resigned.

"Would I be overstepping my bounds if I asked why you're out here?"

She studies me for a moment or two, as if trying to decide if she can trust me. Her eyes narrow and finally she breathes out a long breath. "You were a man of the cloth before, yes?"

"Yes, I was."

"But you've fallen from grace."

"I did, yes."

She drums her fingers across the stump of the tree below her. "How do you live with yourself after you betrayed your deepest beliefs?"

Reassured, I step forward. She isn't trying to be unkind or pass judgment on me. She merely needs guidance and encouragement that she's on a righteous path—that the things we ask of her won't make her a bad person. I can certainly relate to that.

Reaching out to her, I push a loose strand of her platinum locks behind one ear. Much to my surprise, she doesn't shrink back from my touch. Instead, she closes her lovely blue eyes for a moment, and I wonder if I'm soothing her. I hope I am. When she reopens them, they're still moist, and the tears are ready to spill over.

God and goddess, but she's so tiny, like a wisp

from a Sweetland floss bush. I must resist the urge to snatch her up and tuck her safely in my arms because I suddenly feel the strangest sense of protection well up within me. It's quite a silly feeling because a Chosen One doesn't need my protection at all. Every one of them possesses a strength I can never hope to attain. But this isn't about strength. It's about providing comfort when one needs it and that is certainly something I can do.

I reach out and brush away a tear from her eye before it rolls down her face. "It's okay to be upset," I say softly, hoping desperately to soothe her. "Cry if you must. I do the same thing whenever I feel lost or as though I'm not being true to myself and my quest in this life."

"What?" she replies in surprise. "You cry?" She seems taken aback as I nod. "I find that extremely hard to believe," she continues, then narrows those beautiful eyes on me and the suspicion returns to her gaze.

"I suppose I wouldn't believe me either, if I were you," I answer, letting a little chuckle pass my lips. "But, yes, even men are allowed tears when they feel need of them."

She nods and drops her head. "I'm sorry—I didn't mean to imply there's no nobility in a man crying— there certainly is." She looks up at me then. "Every person has a right to his or her own true feelings."

I nod because I agree. "You and I aren't so different."

"We aren't?"

I shake my head. "We both feel deeply, and we've both been thrust into a role we can scarcely bear upon our own two shoulders." She nods fiercely at this. "And we both rely on our tools of the trade to bring their own form of reassurance and calm," I continue, motioning to the crook in her hand. She looks at me with confusion and I realize I need to further explain. "In my case, those tools are in the form of my stole, my sacred text, and other assorted holy items. In weighty times, I find solace in the simplest of things—in washing my vials of holy water and polishing my crucifix. I find that such routine maintenance reassures me, and reminds me of all the reasons I do what I do."

Her curiosity overtakes her apparent grief. "When you belonged to the church, what kind of priest were you?"

"As I said, I was in service to the Church of the Seven Joys. I held the position of supplicant to the god, Morningstar."

"Morningstar? As in—"

I drop my eyes and feel the familiar feelings of shame as they push down upon my shoulders. I wonder if this feeling will ever pass? I hope, within time, it does. "The same you are fated to battle, yes."

She appears aghast, as well she should, given the evil monster Morningstar is. "Why would you ever decide to serve him?"

I frown, not because I'm angry with her, but because I've so often been asked that same question. I've so often asked it of myself. "That was in another life," I respond on a sigh. "Many have changed points of view and sides since then. Suffice to say, I learned some hard lessons and subsequently now serve better masters."

"Maybe not all of us are meant to serve a master, be they better or otherwise," she says on a shrug. "Maybe I was doing what I was supposed to do before I got dragged unwillingly into a battle I know I can't win."

"Oh, Bowie," I sigh as I trace a line across her forehead and smile down at her in a way that I hope betrays my sincerity. She doesn't pull away from my touch. On the contrary, she leans into it and I cup the side of her face as she looks up at me. Her doe eyes are so innocent, so full of kindness—I wonder how she can accomplish what Dolion expects of her... what we all expect of her. "I know you have your doubts about the mission, your abilities, and all of us who accompany you on this journey." I look toward the empty space she was addressing before. "I'd wager you do too, Mr. Sinbad."

She looks up at the spot and makes a face. "You don't want to know what he just said back to you."

I chuckle and then say, "My point is, this is all a perfectly natural reaction. Those who refuse to question their purpose and whether that purpose serves their existing path are more often the most tragic heroes in the end."

"Is that why you stopped serving Morningstar? You realized you didn't question things enough?"

"I suppose I didn't." I hum as I ponder her question with more thought and I continue to rub her cheek with the pad of my thumb. She seems to welcome my touch. "Perhaps it's better if I demonstrate by way of a passage from my old faith. Or are you not in the mood to laugh?"

"Laugh?" she asks, and the dubious look on her face reflects her confusion.

"It's a devotional to Morningstar, himself, disguised in Wonderland gibberish."

"Why would you recite something so silly?"

My face darkens a little as the memories come to the forefront. I have certainly done things for which I'm not proud, but the beauty of life is atonement—I can make up for all the evil deeds of my past and that is exactly what I'm doing now. "Pity."

"For whom?"

"Morningstar, of course."

"Morningstar?" she asks and pulls away from my touch. I allow my hand to fall to my side as I exhale my own interior torment.

"His tale is actually quite tragic. Most people outside the Church of the Seven Joys don't know the truth behind the reality of what made Morningstar the monster he is."

"That sounds like something I might need to hear, then."

"I agree." Before I can begin, though, the sounds of shouts from the camp cut my words short. "Ah, it would seem our absence has finally been noticed."

She begins grabbing her collection of things. "Then we'd better return."

I help her put her supplies back into her pack. She lifts her lantern and leads us back to the camp.

"I promise to tell you that story soon," I say as we walk. "Before we reach the battlefield."

She nods, stopping a moment to give me a breathtakingly beautiful smile. Really, the woman is beyond lovely—something a man of the cloth shouldn't even notice, but I'm afraid I can't help it.

And you are no longer a man of the cloth, Claude, I remind myself.

"I'm looking forward to it," she whispers before resuming her trek.

When we return to the fireside, Dolion comes out of the dark with an anxious look on his face. "Is everything all right?" he asks in that oh-so-serious tone I've come to know so well.

"Quite," I reassure him. "Ms. Bowie just needed a bit of… reflection."

"Ah, good, good," Dolion says, visibly relaxing. "I happened to be up myself and went to check on her, when I saw her tent was empty…"

He doesn't need to say anything else. "Does Jack share your alarm?"

He snorts. "Jack hasn't even woken up, so I'd say not."

"Well, I'm going back to bed," Bowie announces before disappearing into her tent again. When Dolion opens his mouth—most likely to reprimand her, I hold up a finger and shake my head. Whatever he has to say next doesn't need to be said.

When silence overcomes her tent ten or so minutes later, I look up at Dolion, surprised to see he hasn't attempted to retire to his own tent. Clearly, he wants to discuss what just passed between Bowie and me. I'm not surprised—a good captain needs to be in the know at all times.

"How is she really?" Dolion whispers.

"She'll be fine, I think," I reply. "She's just struggling to accept her part in this."

"It's crucial she," he starts but I interrupt, shaking my head.

"You are preaching to the choir, Dolion." He nods as I continue. "You should find your rest before the dawning of the morn."

"I won't be able to sleep."

"You worry too much," I admonish him.

"And I think you and Jack don't worry enough."

"Try to see it from Bowie's perspective," I patiently mutter. "One minute, she's leading a lost soul to the afterlife. The next, we inform her she's been chosen to send a substantial number of men to the afterlife by violent means. That can't be easy for anyone to hear. Especially someone who's anything but battle-worn." I glance at her tent. "Talking to her just now, I find myself at odds with doing what I know we must." I look back at him. "She's not a killer."

"And you think I don't feel the same way?" Dolion asks me with an edge of accusation. It's an interesting question because I don't believe he feels the same way, no. I believe he's so attuned to his cause, that's all he can see.

"Did I say such was what I believed?" I challenge him—he can certainly be difficult, especially when one disagrees with him.

He grunts. "Forgive me my bad temper, but the fact remains. If Bowie doesn't do what she must, more innocent lives will be lost. We can't let her lose sight of that."

"I shall do my part," I tell him. "And I know you and Jack will do yours. She'll just need extra support because this isn't an easy weight for any one person to carry."

He nods, but still looks worried. I interrupt his thoughts, saying, "It's been an equally long day for me, so I shall leave you in search of my own repose. We will talk again tomorrow."

"Tomorrow," he replies. He's still standing by the fire when I return to my tent.

Despite my exhaustion, I lie awake and think about our newest companion.

I can still feel the softness of her skin against my fingertips and smell that perfume of her hair. She's so sweet, refreshingly innocent. How can we ask her to become something she clearly doesn't want to be and, dare I say it, really shouldn't be? How is this her destiny?

I know the answers, of course. We simply must. But the truth still doesn't sit well with me.

I, of all people, know how cunning Morningstar can be. His threat to Fantasia goes far beyond the power of his magic or his raw enchantment. He's deceitful and as wretchedly cunning as they come. He'll stop at nothing to have his way, using whatever pawns and tools he requires to end the lives of anyone who dares to cross him.

I sometimes wonder if the prophecy is merely a ploy by Morningstar to churn up false hope. Could he have a larger scheme afoot that we won't discover until it's too late? That, however, doesn't square with what we know of his plans.

According to Dolion, all the Chosen Ones are on Morningstar's death list. In response, the Guild has commissioned a number of people to retrieve each and every Chosen One to do what we are doing: protecting them as they prepare for the final battle. Of course, if captured by Morningstar, he wouldn't think twice about killing any of them, not even someone as sweet and innocent as Bowie. As much as I loathe what we're doing in forcing her to destroy so many people, this is her fate—her reason for being—and we must protect her day and night.

Indeed, I believe Morningstar already knows one of the Chosen is a shepherd. That would certainly explain why so many of the shepherds have vanished lately. But with all the potions and spells he uses to cloud the minds of his minions—who call themselves his 'devoted servants'—it's more than difficult to determine what Morningstar is up to.

Having spent so long in his employ, I know that for a fact. He bends the minds of others to do his evil will and corrupts them to see him as some sort of terrible mythic figure. But when the layers of hypocrisy are peeled away, he is no more than a pathetically lost and sad man. He's constantly fighting to regain control of those within his lead, and every motive he has is a selfish one. Employing people like Hassan demonstrates how far he's willing to go in order to get his way.

Mind, recent whispers claim that Hassan was banished from the Caves of Larne in the Anoka Desert. But as no one can confirm such rumors, I treat that information as nothing better than idle gossip. It may be true, but we've no way of proving it. The one thing above all I know to be true: Morningstar is the most dangerous being in this realm, and he's intent on widespread destruction at all costs.

Chapter Six
Jack

"Bowie, are you awake?" I call through the front of her tent, careful to remain outside in case she's not fully dressed. Though, of course I would love to witness her nudity, I do try to at least appear somewhat civilized, regardless of the fact that I'm an uncouth beast underneath it all. And, yes, I have imagined Bowie naked and underneath me on more than one occasion.

"I am now," she grumbles from inside.

"My apologies for waking you so early, but we have much to accomplish."

"You mean we aren't continuing to march towards the battlefield?"

"Dolion would insist otherwise, but I convinced him that we can take an extra day. We're secure enough now, in this forest, to begin your first lesson."

"Fine, I'll be out shortly," she replies amicably.

Even though I wasn't awake the evening before, word is that she attempted to escape, but Claude was able to reason with her—which is fortunate. If Claude is good at anything, it's the spoken word. I, myself,

65

tend more towards silence as I believe actions far outweigh the value of words.

"Sooner is always better," I respond.

A few moments later, she crawls out of her tent. She looks a bit disheveled, but she's still stunningly beautiful. She makes such a perfect vision, I have to avert my eyes. There's no time for the business of admiration… not for any of us. And especially not for an uncivilized barbarian such as myself. I have no business being in the company of a lady, let alone one of the Chosen. But that doesn't mean I don't want to bed her—maybe the fact that she's a lady makes me want her all the more? To dirty her body and prove to her she's no better than me.

Rein it in, Jack, I admonish myself.

I notice, with amusement, that not one of us can stop staring at her when she enters our vicinity. Even the spirit, Sinbad, whom I sometimes catch glimpses of, follows her with his eyes wherever she goes. Not only do we all watch her, but we watch her as the wolf watches the rabbit—with hunger. Even the ever-faithful Claude watches her with lust-filled eyes.

Claude claims to be a man of the cloth, but he's actually a *former* man of the cloth, thus I suppose he isn't tied to the rules he once was—rules of abstinence. It's hard to define what he is or isn't when we've all been forced to form new allegiances and thus, take on new roles. Regardless, he remains a red-blooded man like any other, and he's obviously noticed the beauty nestled among us. I can't help but wonder whether the good man enjoyed any of Bowie's… *favors* during his clandestine rendezvous with her last night. At the thought, a strange feeling of jealousy rises through me and it's all I can do to stamp those fires out.

I am not a jealous man, by nature, and the feeling is foreign to me. Furthermore, I don't like it.

While Claude's interest in Bowie and her obvious beauty doesn't surprise me, Dolion's does. For the first time in all our travels that I can recall, I find him looking at a woman the way Claude and I do. In the past, his little interest in any woman, however beautiful, made me wonder if he might prefer men. Such a preference is fine by me though I, myself, am only attracted to the fairer sex, but Bowie seems to contradict my hypothesis where Dolion is concerned.

I can't say whether it's simply Bowie's good looks or something else that draws us to her so magnetically. She's a contrast and a paradox. At first glance, she appears so tiny that a strong breeze might blow her away. But I quickly learn it's a grave mistake to underestimate her or consider her weak in any way.

When we begin our lessons, the power inside her small frame is astounding, and she's barely begun to tap into it. The only problem I perceive is she doesn't seem very eager to push herself. Is she afraid of her power? Or is she afraid of what will be expected of her if she utilizes it? I have a feeling it's the latter.

I sometimes wonder if the soul stone made a mistake in marking her as a Chosen One—there's just nothing outwardly powerful about her—she's just a slip of a thing. However, I know that's not possible. The stones are always conclusive. That being said, I'm unimpressed with Bowie's efforts in her training, at this point. It seems she's uninterested in trying—in excelling or proving herself. Because I'm spurred by competition, I don't understand her. And I'm fairly sure she doesn't understand me—it's as though we speak different languages. Regardless, if she doesn't try harder, she'll quickly perish on the actual field of battle.

"You must push yourself harder, Bowie," I repeat after the tenth underwhelming performance. I'm attempting to bring her magic to the fore—to infiltrate her fingertips in order to lift a handful of leaves from the forest floor. So far, the leaves haven't so much as moved.

"I didn't ask for this job," she complains, throwing her hands on her hips as she turns to glare at me.

"Irrelevant. Your task must be done by you and you alone. You're the Chosen One, after all."

"Well, I didn't ask for that title either," she gripes again.

"Yet it was thrust on you," I answer, not appreciating her tone or the fact that she's feeling sorry for herself. Chosen shouldn't feel sorry for themselves. "And like all the other Chosen Ones, you must do what's expected of you."

"But *why* must I?" she demands, throwing her crook to the ground. She's pouting now. Most unbecoming of any pupil of magic. "Why can't the rest of the Chosen handle it by themselves? Or are they as weak as I am?"

"They're honing their skills just like we're developing yours. While I can't attest to the current levels of their expertise, I do know some have already accomplished very impressive feats."

"Such as?"

I cock my head to the side. "The Seelie Princess, Tinker, single-handedly almost killed the Unseelie King! It's a promising start."

"And how much more promising if she could've taken him down once and for all!"

"I agree, but she's still learning to master her powers, just as you are."

"I doubt I have much to master."

"Only because you're restraining yourself!" I snap in response, irritated with her foul mood, which seems to only make mine even more so. "As long as you insist on refusing to push yourself, you'll never realize your true potential."

She responds with a sour look and crosses her arms against her ample breasts. Gods! How foolishly stubborn this shepherdess is! Claude's advice to rely on patience and a nurturing approach is clearly not working. Of course, he's much more patient than I am by rule, but this is just beyond frustrating.

Regardless, I'm not sure how to handle Bowie. I can't use the usual approach I would take with a man—forcefulness. I'm trying to keep my cool, trying to be understanding, but her adamant refusal to stretch her powers any further than what little she's demonstrated so far is purely exasperating. She needs motivation, but so far that motivation isn't being created by kind words.

What happened to the girl who stormed off into her tent in a fit of rage on our first night at camp? She's the one I need right now—I need her fire, her anger, her fight. And that's when I realize exactly what I must do. I have to admit, the idea of doing it leaves me chomping at the bit.

"Maybe you're right," I say, my voice changing its tone as I narrow my eyes at her. "Maybe you are *incapable*."

She seems relieved I'm finally agreeing with her. "Yes, exactly what I've been saying all this time... I can't do it."

I grin because I'm sure I'll enjoy the argument that's soon to follow. "I'm beginning to realize as much. You're taking the coward's way out."

She glares at me. "I'm not a coward—I'm just not as capable as you seem to think I am."

"No, I don't believe that's it," I reply, shaking my head. "I believe you're taking the path of the coward simply because you don't want to participate in this battle. You're... afraid."

She blinks in rapid succession and replies with tight lips, "I never said that."

"You don't need to. It's clear in your actions."

"My actions say nothing of the sort."

"Don't they?" I ask, shaking my head as I see the fire begin burning within her eyes—exactly what I was

70

hoping for. And I'm not done yet. "No more of discussing your cowardice," I continue as her blue eyes burn. "Instead, I want to discuss this spirit of yours."

"I don't," she answers, glaring at me.

I put my finger on my chin as I wonder how I can more fully command that anger of hers. I have a feeling the spirit is a good course—as soon as I brought him up, her anger turned up a notch. "Do you love him? Is that why you keep him tethered to you and unable to seek his afterlife?"

"Love him? I barely know him," she seethes at me.

"Then it's not love," I study her with a mocking smile. "Sexual desire then?" Her eyes nearly pop right out of her head and I have to keep myself from laughing. "Ah, that must be it. You fancy this dead man."

"You know nothing of what you speak," she spits the words at me. "And I won't dignify your awful comments with a response."

"It does beg a question though…" I continue, pretending not to notice her anger. "Is it even possible to fuck someone who doesn't actually possess a body?"

She gasps, her nostrils flaring with outrage, and she seems at a loss for words.

A calculated chuckle sneaks from my lips. "As if you don't think about that exact topic every night while you lie in bed. You lay there and wonder what it could be like if he were still alive and if he were buried deep between your thighs."

"How dare you!" she snaps, forcing me to duck her

crook when she swings it at my head. "*You're* the reason his journey to the afterlife is taking so long! You're the reason why he's here!"

"I fail to understand."

"Because neither of us fully trusts any of you," she manages, her voice wavering with her anger. "Because he's my... my protector and he won't leave me until he knows I'm safe!"

"Well, if you don't trust us by now, then you should leave," I reply icily, increasing the nasty tone to my voice. "It would be as simple as refusing to fill your role. Take your lost soul to his precious afterlife and be done with it."

"It's not so simple."

"Isn't it?"

"No," she glares at me.

Her head jerks sideways when the shadowy figure of Sinbad appears beside her. I'm surprised because usually none of us can see him. Obviously, he feels the need to respond to my comments or to protect Bowie's modesty. I can't let his words disrupt my progress with Bowie, though. It's time to move in for the kill.

"Has your pet spirit come to protect you? To stand up to my truths?" I jibe.

"Shut up!" she shouts. "You have no idea what you're talking about!"

"Maybe I do and maybe I don't." I focus on the spirit, but I can't make out his features. He just appears as a shadow beside her. That's when I think of another tactic. I face Bowie again. "Actually, I can help you more than you might believe."

She looks at me then and pauses. "What do you mean?"

"I can help you dispatch your spirit."

"Dispatch him?"

I nod. "I'm just as capable of sending your lost soul to his afterlife as you are—via my magic. Though I would do so in a much more… direct route."

"Don't you dare!"

"Why not? You just said we interrupted your journey in getting him to his ever after. Thus, I'd be more than happy to help both of you by returning him to the exact place he's supposed to go."

Her head jerks sideways again, and she cocks her ear to listen closely to what Sinbad is saying. She's seething, but she hasn't quite lost control of herself… yet. So, I must now turn to my own magic. I intend to make her dead friend visible to me so I can fully understand the relationship between them and the control he has over her, if any.

"Come, Spirit, let's get you to the other side," I say as I face the shadow and hold up my hands. As Sinbad begins to take shape, I feel the tingle of Bowie's power rising to challenge mine. I extend my fingers and summoning my magic between them, I fling a bolt of light (that isn't meant to do anything) in the ghost's direction when a blast of power bursts forth from Bowie's crook. The bolt of energy knocks me backwards, launching me through the air.

I climb to my feet and look around with a slow

smile. It's exactly as I knew it would be—Bowie possesses power and then some.

Claude and Dolion are suddenly nearby, both are wearing thrilled expressions. The entire clearing around Bowie and me is charred and black. Excluding us, every other living thing that formerly existed here—trees, grass, birds, squirrels—lies dead from the blast of her crook. I finally have my proof that her power is tremendous, but she's still unfocused. If she'd concentrated her power more directly at me, she most certainly would have killed me.

Regardless, it's a promising start!

Bowie, however, isn't thrilled with her results.

She takes a step toward me and, then pulling back her arm, hits me across the face with her small hand. Of course, the slap doesn't do more than sting slightly.

"You... bastard!" she yells, emphasizing each word with a sharp blow. I hold my smarting cheek and chuckle down at her as she glares up at me. Using her free hand to indicate our now devastated surroundings, she says, "Do you realize I could have shot you into the ether with that blast?"

"Does that mean you don't want to add me to your spirit harem then?" I reply with a laugh. "Because I thought that was exactly what you were aiming to do."

She continues to glare at me, her whole body shaking with her fury. "That was completely irresponsible of you! Irresponsibility is dangerous." A look of disgust overtakes her, and she turns away from me.

"Where do you think you're going?" Dolion calls after her.

"I'm leaving," she answers. "I've had enough. No matter how worthy the cause, I won't be playing these games with you. I'm escorting Sinbad to the Endless Night and then I'm returning to my post as shepherdess."

I instantly realize I've overplayed my hand. I walk up to her and take her by the shoulder. "Bowie, you need to—"

"I don't need to do anything!" she snaps, throwing my hand off her. "What I *do* need is to complete my job as a shepherdess." She seems mournful. "There're too few of us left as it is, and I've wasted enough of my time here with all of you."

"How many shepherds are currently ferrying souls to the Endless Night?" I demand, gripping her arm and refusing to let go. She's not going anywhere and I'm about to make sure that's so.

"As far as I know, only me," she admits.

"And why do you think that is, Bowie?"

"I don't know," she answers, throwing the words back at me as if they're a curse. "Some illness killed many. A few of them had lethal accidents."

"And how many have been replaced?" I ask.

I can see the wheels turning in her head. "None, as far as I know," she starts again.

"And why might that be?"

"Morningstar," she says, visible dread crossing her face.

75

"Exactly," I tell her. "If Morningstar knows a Chosen One could be hiding among the shepherds, wouldn't he decimate the lot of them, just in case?" I get close enough to her that only a few inches of air separate us. Her eyes instantly widen and I can see the pulse in her neck quickening. I'm making her nervous and, though I'm unsure why, I like that fact. "How long before he learns there's only one shepherd alive? How long before he comes for you?" She's shaking now as the full weight of my words bears down on her slight shoulders. "So," I add, "still want to go back to where you came from?"

She pulls her arm back and slaps me again. Tears reflect in her eyes as she turns on her toes and immediately starts for the camp. Obviously, she hates me, but I don't care. I've done what I needed to do in order to make sure she doesn't try to escape. I've made her understand there is no escape.

Claude starts past me and gives me a sour look of reproach. "That was a cruel and foolish thing to say," he comments as he follows her. Still the caretaker at heart, even without his robes.

"That was the most encouraging sign of progress I've seen in the last several days," Dolion chirps with a wry smile as he claps me on the back. "Keep up the excellent work!"

"I wonder if there's a limit as to how far we can push her," I reply, watching her intently as she marches forward and Claude does his best to catch up to her. "She wasn't wrong about how dangerous my first ploy was."

"Perhaps, but we have no other choice. We need her cooperation; she doesn't have to like us."

I stare at Dolion. "Even for you, isn't that a bit cold?"

"War is much colder. So are death and destruction." He waves his hand at the blackened results of Bowie's magic. "All of this is a mere sample of what will happen if Morningstar prevails. That's why we need Bowie to do her part."

"Which I obviously understand or I wouldn't have done what I did," I point out.

His expression softens somewhat. "I know, my friend, but we can't lose sight of how important this is."

"Then I'll keep at it," I assure him. "Perhaps she'll come around, eventually."

"The sooner she does, the better," he replies, walking away.

I watch him disappear down the path to our camp. After a last look at what Bowie accomplished this afternoon, I sigh. Then I wave my hands around me in wide circles, summoning the power of the earth. The charred area begins to brighten with fresh color. Green grass springs up from the barren ground. Bark and leaves on the nearby trees regrow until they're as alive as they ever were. Even the birds and squirrels are resurrected from what would have been a terminal slumber.

With the damage restored, I return to camp.

On previous nights, Bowie told us stories around

77

the campfire to help pass the time. They were mostly outlandish tales relayed to her by her phantom friend. I fear we might miss hearing about our epic adventure this night. Or perhaps, ever again.

Chapter Seven
Bowie

My feet are as heavy as lead, shaking the earth with each step as I angrily stomp toward my tent. Sinbad floats right beside me, his body often passing through bushes and other obstacles. He barely glances at them as if they do no more than tickle his aura.

"How dare he threaten you like that," I say to him, my temper still hot from the whole pitiful exercise.

"I said he was bluffing you from the start," Sinbad patiently counters, shaking his head. "But had he been asked to make good on his threat, it would have been fine."

"Would it?" I inquire, looking at him with genuine fear. "What if he actually meant what he said?"

"It is what it is."

That further angers me. "You won't allow me to take you across the threshold, but it's okay if he does it?"

"He had no intention of doing it," Sinbad insists, shrugging. "He was speaking nonsense, and he knew it. The only thing he accomplished was to make me more visible. That's a far cry from sending me away from

79

here."

While I believe him, his logic fails to settle my nerves. "He might still do it yet. If I hadn't stopped him…"

He releases a frustrated sigh. "Round and round, your thoughts chase themselves. I was never his concern, Bowie. You are. That's why he provoked your anger."

"For what purpose?"

"I'd think it should be obvious…"

"Well, play along with me for a moment and pretend it isn't obvious!" I don't mean to yell at him, but can't help it. I'm just so angry!

He smiles at me and I take a deep breath, quickly apologizing, to which he just nods.

"Jack was trying to get the exact response from you that he did," Sinbad continues. "He knew you were keeping yourself under restraint."

"So why do that to me? Why provoke me?"

"To teach you how to focus your power properly, Jack must first know what you're capable of. He even told you that, but you refused to listen."

"I don't want this—any of it!" I cry, tears rolling down my face. "I don't want these powers! None of them!" I'm so upset, I almost ignore the tent flap being pushed back as someone steps inside. I blink away my tears and turn to see that it's Claude.

"What happened, Bowie?" he asks in alarm and opens his arms wide, as if to welcome me. I don't know why I do, but I hurry towards him, allowing him to pull

me into a hug. He just feels somehow safe to me—and I
believe, deep down, that Claude truly cares about me.
He's the only one of the bunch that I can trust, the only
who actually gives a damn about me.

"I don't want this, Claude," I whisper. "I don't
want to be here. I don't feel like I'm supposed to be
here. I'm no hero. I just want to return to the Mallow
Fields and do the job I was doing."

"Shh," he croons into my ear and strokes my hair
as I cry into his chest.

I look up at him and shake my head. "This isn't for
me. Violence and war… it just… it feels so wrong."

"Easy, easy," he murmurs. "First, take a deep
breath."

"I don't want to be here any longer," I repeat. How
strange that his touch seems to settle my nerves like a
mother calms a child. I hold on to him even harder and
he responds by tightening his arms around me. It's
strange, but I'm suddenly overcome with the need to
kiss him, to taste his lips. Of course, I stifle the need
and instead, focus on the fact that I hate Jack with all
my being.

"Bowie, you were made for this singular purpose,"
Claude says softly. "I know it feels like a huge weight
to bear, but perhaps you can choose to see it in another
light?"

"Another light?" I laugh without humor, shaking
my head.

He nods, and his smile is warm, kind. "You're a
Chosen One. That means you're one of the very few

81

who *can* do this."

"But I can't!"

"Yes, you can," he argues gently, holding me tighter to his chest. "I believe in you. So does Dolion, although he'll never admit it. And so does Jack."

"Jack," I repeat his name like a curse.

"Yes, I'm very familiar with his methods and seeing how distraught you are, I can only assume he's pushed you too far."

"He's an awful, mean—" I start.

"Shh," Claude quiets me. "Jack is many things, but his intentions are in the right place, though it may not seem like it now."

I shake my head. "How can you stand to travel with them? You're nothing like they are."

"Because we are all united under the same common goal, Bowie. And that same goal includes you, too."

"I just… I don't feel like it should include me. I still feel like there's been some sort of mistake."

"There's no mistake," Claude chuckles. "And the point remains: Bowie, you *can* do this! It's time for you to believe in yourself." He takes a breath. "Look at what you were able to do when your magic was triggered. Your power is… incomprehensible, really."

I look up at him, wishing I *could* believe everything he says, but I'm still unable to. I can't wrap my head around it yet. It's too much to take in. I feel just like the first night I camped with them, desperate to turn around and run away. I wish I were as far away from this place and these men as I could possibly be. Let someone else battle for Fantasia! My only responsibility should be escorting lost souls to the afterlife.

Dolion steps into the tent then, prompting me to shrink away from Claude and take refuge as far from Dolion as I can get. If Jack comes into my tent, I will leave.

"Bowie…" Dolion begins.

"Before you voice that thought," Claude tells him with a note of reproach, "try to keep in mind that she's still reeling from Jack's rather draconian teaching methods."

For the first time, the man who snatched me off the street refuses to meet my eyes. "We both know it had to be done."

"Do we?" I retort. "Or are you trying to make me into something I'm not?"

"Come now, Bowie," Dolion says in exasperation, shaking his head. "You saw what you're capable of. You saw the power that burst from within you."

"That doesn't mean anything," I insist. "I can't control it."

"And that's exactly what Jack is trying to teach you," Dolion argues. "He wants to teach you how to control it."

"It doesn't change the fact that I want no part of this."

"You are one of the few that can lead us to victory and defeat Morningstar once and for all."

I can see he's trying to make amends, but I don't trust him. I look up at Claude, the only one I do trust, and he nods, patting my arm. He tacitly encourages me to listen to Dolion.

"Your assets are as potent and sharp as any blade," Dolion continues. "Use them to save the lives of the people who would otherwise perish. They must depend on you and the other Chosen to fight for them because they can't fight for themselves. Only you can protect them, Bowie. That's your role and following your destiny as the Fates dictate will make all the difference in the world, believe me." He takes my hand and gives it a gentle but firm squeeze. I don't pull it away. "Please believe me."

For a moment, I don't know what to think. His praise, though unsolicited, emboldens me. And his words are kinder than I thought him capable. Maybe these men aren't as bad as I think they are? Well, I know Claude is a good man, certainly. Could it follow that Dolion must also be a good man—since Claude believes in him?

I look at Dolion and study him for a few seconds.

"Can we make amends?" he asks. He holds out his hand and I look down at it. Then a second later, I accept his hand and he pulls me into the heat of his body, wrapping his arms around me, just as Claude was holding me earlier. I'm surprised because Dolion and I don't have a relationship like this—at least, I didn't think we did. But maybe this is his way of saying we're on the same side—that we're fighting the same enemy.

I look up and him and, strangely, I feel compelled to kiss him, just as I felt compelled to kiss Claude earlier. What in the blazes is wrong with me? I don't understand these strange feelings of desire that seem to be surging up within me lately and at the most inopportune moments.

Dolion doesn't seem surprised by the expression in my eyes, but wraps his arms around me and pulls me closer. It soothes me at once and feels right somehow. I wish my powers felt as right as this feeling does. I'm vaguely aware of Claude discreetly exiting my tent. Sinbad is still lingering nearby, but I ignore him. I need Dolion's warm touch. I need the warmth of another human right now—someone who can hold me and tell me everything is going to be okay. I want to forget everything else except how it feels to be a woman in the arms of a man.

Suddenly, my brain starts working again and I realize how easily swayed I am by someone I would never call my friend. Just moments ago, I hated Dolion almost as much as I hated Jack and now, I'm resting in his arms and contemplating kissing him? What is wrong with me?

I quickly pull away from him and decide I need some fresh air—my mind is just a tumultuous heap of thoughts and my emotions are wreaking havoc with me.

I step away from him and duck outside the tent flap, breathing in deeply. Then I start walking for the forest, needing to be alone. I don't look back to see if Dolion follows me, but because I can't hear the sound of his footsteps, I figure he doesn't.

"So," Sinbad says when he floats up beside me, "are you ready to continue training?"

"No," I tell him. "Not after I almost killed my tutor."

Sinbad chuckles as he smiles down at me. "Well, in lieu of looking for Jack then," he says as he sits down, or, more accurately, floats above the ground in a seated position. "How about a new story?"

"How many stories do you have?" I ask as I take a seat on the forest floor and lean against one of the many trees, exhaling out all my frustration.

"Hard to say. There are so many."

"If you had to estimate, what number would you guess?"

He shrugs. "Maybe a thousand? A thousand and one?"

I scoff. "That number is as exaggerated as your stories are."

"Hardly. I'm just a simple seaman with a wealth of experience on the many seas I've sailed."

I frown at him. "So, you're saying all these stories are factual?"

He shrugs. "You must be the ultimate judge in the end."

I hum, suggesting that I remain unconvinced. But, deep down, I'm beyond grateful for Sinbad's company… and his… friendship. Yes, 'friendship' is exactly what I would call it, strange though it might be. "All right, let's hear the story then, Sinbad."

I listen to his magical tale about a great war on the high seas that pitted fierce pirates against clever merchants. Their ammunition for war depleted, they began using whatever they had on hand or could find to weaponize. Resorting to a cache of potatoes from the galley, they lobbed the silly things at one another's ships, aiming for maximum carnage. And, thus, Sinbad successfully illustrates the futility of war.

Sinbad soon has me in stitches and I temporarily forget the trials and tribulations of the day. After I've had enough fresh air, I crawl back into my tent and listen as Sinbad launches into a little dirge he learned on his many voyages. Fairly soon, I gradually nod off to sleep.

Chapter Eight
Sinbad

Freedom from sleep has both its good and bad points.

On one hand, it can be rather tiresome to hover about all the time, staying wide awake for hours with nothing to do and no company to distract me. On the other hand, I can watch Bowie while she sleeps. Although I can't protect her in my ghostly state, I can certainly warn her of imminent danger.

One potential danger becomes apparent from time to time: a man just as restless as I am. Dolion.

He also watches Bowie while she sleeps, but his is not an expression of love or longing. Rather, it's a blank stare, the gaze of a man scheming. I wonder what's on his mind. There's something about him that bothers me; something I've yet to identify. But I'm fairly certain he has dark secrets. Men like us always bear secrets, usually because those secrets aren't fit to share with the world. But what I sense from Dolion is much bleaker and more sinister.

As strange as it sounds, I fear—as with all commanders—that to him, Bowie is no more than a necessary tool for battle. I wouldn't be surprised in the slightest if her encounter with him earlier was conveniently planned and not in the heat of the moment, as she probably assumes. It might even be his latest ruse to persuade her to do his bidding. Few men can command armies without first becoming masters of manipulation.

And he is definitely intent on manipulating her—both into battle and into his bed. I'm no fool—I've seen the way he looks at her with a desire that seems to eat him from the inside out. It's different to the desire in Claude's eyes or in Jack's. Claude's is the sort of desire that leads me to believe he's falling in love with her and Jack... well, that sort of desire is of the purely carnal sort at the moment. He wants to bed her, even though she angers him. Clearly, she's gotten underneath his skin.

Yet, Dolion...

I wish I were still alive so I could interrogate him. I know a number of methods that would make him sing like a lark, and reveal his true intentions. Moments of longing like these make me the saddest about being dead. Perhaps Bowie is right. Once we fulfill her purpose, it might be time for me to cross over, leaving her behind, and possibly never seeing her again in my next life. The thought of such a permanent parting actually depresses me quite a bit.

As odd as it might sound, I've grown quite attached to the shepherdess. And I'm more than aware that she's become increasingly attached to me. It's as if we're all we've got in this forest of darkness and with these strangers neither of us can trust.

Perhaps the only one we can trust is Claude—there's something about him that reveals he's a man of his word—someone honest and true. Jack is a question mark—he's harsh, yes, but that doesn't make him a bad person.

It's Dolion that causes me the most chagrin, because I can't see beyond the carefully constructed mask he wears.

Currently, I watch Dolion so intently that I'm startled when Bowie screams out in terror. She bolts upright to face him, which leads me to guess she spotted him spying on her. But when I see the look of pure terror on her face, I know differently. Whatever frightened her could only have come from her own psyche. She had a nightmare, is my guess. But before I can offer some much-needed words of comfort, she spots Dolion looking at her through the open tent flap.

"What are you doing?" she demands.

"I heard you scream," he lies.

"He's been staring at you intermittently all night," I whisper into her ear. I've no idea if the shadows hide me at the moment, but I can't really say I care. She needs to know the truth.

"You were already standing there when I awoke, so I doubt that," she says, with no hint that she heard me.

"It wasn't the first time you screamed in your sleep," Dolion continues to lie, compounding his deceit.

90

"I heard you scream earlier and came to inquire what was wrong. But you were still asleep when I arrived."

"More lies," I tell her. "You haven't stirred once until now."

The way she cocks her head ever so slightly, I know she hears my words. Stirring from her covers, she stands up and moves toward him. He reaches out, as if to comfort her, placing his hands on her shoulders. He looks deeply into her eyes as she looks up at him and as I watch, he shifts his hands down from her shoulders to her breasts, which are much more noticeable in her shift. Her nipples protrude through the light fabric and as I watch in anger and jealousy, Dolion runs his fingers past the nubs, immediately causing them to harden.

The expression on Bowie's face is unreadable and when I believe she's about to give into him, much to his surprise, she simply knees him hard between his legs, shoving his hands away before pushing past him.

"Don't touch me," she growls as she hurries past him and keeps walking towards the woods that surround the camp. I follow her with all haste, my faded body passing through Dolion, who struggles to recover from the blow to his manhood. His eyebrows shoot up with frightened awareness when I pass right through him, making him look around as if he felt me but can't explain what I was.

Does he feel me? I wonder as something else then occurs to me—something I can't explain. *Why was he so cold when I passed through him? Is that what the living are supposed to feel like?*

As interesting as the answers to these questions might be, I have more pressing matters to deal with at the moment. I flutter through the trees, watching the leaves and branches as they appear through my skin as I go.

I find Bowie in a clearing. She stands there and stares out at the dark forest as if it has answers for her—answers as to why she's here and whether or not she can trust the men with her. Of course, the forest has no answers. Only silence.

"What are you doing?" I ask her.

"What does it look like I'm doing?" she snaps.

"Plotting to run away?"

"No," she answers.

"I thought…" I start and then I'm not sure how to say the rest of the words. "I thought you were going to give yourself to him back there."

She nods and swallows hard. "I thought the same thing for a second or two." Then she turns to look at me and breathes in deeply. "I can't explain it, but I feel as if Dolion… has this… power over me." She looks out at the darkness another few seconds before she drops her head and then sighs out her despondency. "You must think I'm silly."

"No. I think you're in a situation you don't like, but you can't see that there's any way out of it."

"That about sums it up," she answers on a smile. Then she sighs again. "I keep having these vivid nightmares, Sinbad. But I suppose that's all they are."

She looks over at me. "Nightmares."

"So I saw."

"You witnessed me having the nightmare?"

I nod. "I'm afraid I have no need for sleep." Then I clear my throat even though I don't need to—it's just one of those comforting things that reminds me of when I was alive. "I am, after all, your protector."

She wears a reluctant smile. "If you were Dolion, Claude or Jack, I'd think you watching me was creepy. But because it's you, I find it sweet."

My poor, dead heart swells with emotion. "I can't deny feeling flattered."

She looks up at me, and her expression is sweet. "You really do care about me, don't you, Sinbad?"

For once, I have no witty remark or glib deflection to bandy back. It's a question I've not dared ask myself. A dead man has no business loving a live, vibrant woman like her. "Would it help if you told me about your nightmare?"

At first, she seems reluctant. Then she clears her throat and nods, saying, "It's always the same. I'm a little girl being chased by something huge and horrible. I can't see it, but I know it's there. Then the nightmare changes and I watch as my skull explodes and blood and brain matter and fragments of bone shoot onto the ground all around me." She shudders. "It's as if my head spontaneously bursts open like a pustule."

I float nearer to her. "What a horrible thing to dream!"

"That's not all of it," she replies. "While I'm lying

93

there, with my head splattered all over the ground, something lifts me up and carries me away."

Even by the loose logic of dreams, that makes little sense. "But you're dead."

"No, I'm not." She shakes her head and explains, "I know I should be dead, but somehow I'm still alive." Her face grows sad. "I haven't had that dream for quite a while. Until tonight, I was sure it was an ugly phase of my childhood."

"Perhaps it was due to your extremely stressful day. The nightmare crept into an opening so it could ambush you once more."

She smiles again as she fully turns to face me. "I think maybe you're right."

"Just remember this," I say, "it's only a dream, a phantasm of the night, with no true substance. It's not a real danger in this world, which I will always protect you from as long as I can."

Her smile widens and I've no doubt that she'd hug me if she could. "I know you will." She walks back toward me.

Out of reflex, I reach out to her, attempting to put my hand on her shoulder. But of course, it only passes through her flesh. When I feel the sensations of her body, I pull my hand away rapidly. Going by the surprised look on her face, she feels it too. Unlike Dolion, she's warm. That leads me to a conundrum I can't parse: which is normal? Bowie's warmth or Dolion's coldness? Which is the normal sensation I create when I travel through a living being?

"I… I apologize," I tell her, concealing my discomfort. "I tried to comfort you but—"

"No, it's all right," she assures me. "That felt… good." She suddenly seems shy. "Almost intimate."

Encouraged, I put both hands on her shoulders. The warmth I draw from her is undeniable. A wonderful exchange of energy passes between us. It's almost the feeling of orgasm—something carnal and filling. I pull away again, but I'm invigorated by the action. When I look at Bowie, her cheeks are flushed and her breathing has picked up.

"Did you feel it too?" I ask.

She merely nods, and I put my hands on her again, this time on her breasts, mimicking what Dolion did earlier. At her swift intake of breath and the way her lips part, I can tell she must feel the same thing I do—pleasure. My mind swirls with countless possibilities.

"We… we should get back," she says, and I have the good sense to say nothing more but to nod and release her. She takes a few steps towards the camp and I follow her.

As we walk, she looks at me with her lips pursed together in a tender expression. "I'm sorry you died."

"So am I," I say with a little chuckle.

Her face threatens to become a frown. "No, I don't mean it like that. It's just…" She loses her train of thought and I wonder if she's at a loss for words or if she's embarrassed by what she nearly said. Either way, I want to know what's on her mind.

"Take your time, Bowie," I reassure her. "I have

nothing but time, so no reason to hurry."

Her frown dissipates at this. "I wish I could have met you when you were alive," she says softly and refuses to look at me. "You're the kind of man I believe I could... fall in love with."

How limited such love can ultimately be! But I refrain from telling her that and instead I say, "Though I no longer inhabit my mortal shell, you can still love me as I most certainly love you."

"Do you mean that?"

"Why would I lie?"

"To tell a good story."

I have to laugh at that. "Perhaps. But when it comes to matters of the heart, I never jest."

She suddenly comes to a halt, her eyes widening. "Is something wrong?" I ask. Does my careless impulse offend her?

She stares at me with those lovely eyes. "Do you trust me?"

"Like no one else in this world."

"A moment ago, when you touched me, your hands went... um, right through my body."

"I didn't harm you, did I?" I ask in alarm.

"No, no, nothing like that," she reassures me. "But I could *feel* you, Sinbad. My skin tingled in response and I believe... I believe the feelings between us had something to do with the tether that binds us, our souls. Could you feel me?"

"Yes, I could," I tell her. "You are warm, a feeling I've forgotten already."

"Then remind yourself of that feeling."

I frown. "I'm not sure I follow."

"If you're a spirit, then doesn't it follow that you can inhabit someone's body?" she asks as I nod to say I'm following her line of thinking. "Then inhabit my body."

The full implications of her comment slay me with the force of a battering ram. "Are you saying what I think you're saying?"

"If you think I'm asking you to enter and possess me, then yes," she says excitedly.

We stand there for a moment as I contemplate her generous offer. For the second time in as many minutes, I'm once more at a loss for words.

"Come now, Sinbad," she finally purrs. "After all those great adventures you related by the campfire, surely you aren't worried by something as insignificant as this."

"I don't know, Bowie," I must admit. "I've arguably few scruples. But this seems to conflict with the few I have."

"It's hardly like jumping inside someone who doesn't want you there," she points out. "I'm inviting you inside me."

"And what if it harms you somehow? I don't want to be the cause of—"

"It didn't hurt when your hand went through me. If anything, it tickled a little."

I take a deep breath. Then, before I can talk myself out of it, I step inside her.

97

Chapter Nine
Bowie

When Sinbad steps inside me, it's a feeling like walking into the ocean in the middle of a hot day—a sense of coolness washes over me—coolness charged with electricity. Almost all at once, every fiber of my being feels as if it's been stimulated, washed over with a current of power.

"This feels so strange," I say. It's not uncomfortable, but it also didn't feel like it did when Sinbad merely touched me earlier.

"Am I hurting you?" Sinbad asks in my voice. "If this is painful, I'll exit from your lovely form this instant." Hearing myself speak with his cadence is a little disorienting. It gives new meaning to "talking to myself."

"I know, Sinbad," I say with a smile. "And, no, it doesn't hurt."

"How does it feel for you?" he asks in my voice.

I examine all the sensations in my body. "*Odd* is the best way I can describe it. There's a unique tingle in my body, but I also sense a peaceful sensation coming from you. I compare it to being held by you, but it goes much deeper than that." It feels like being wrapped in a warm embrace. "How do you feel?"

"Warm," he replies in thought, making me smile again. "Like I've come home from a long journey and I'm thawing out beside the fire. I feel happy."

"Yes, that's a good way to describe it."

"Tell me, Bowie," he says. "Can you move independently and free of my will?"

"I think so," I reply before moving my hand upward. Even as I do, I see the action through a pair of inner eyes that weren't there before. They don't belong to me, but I seem to share their unique perspective.

"And what about now?" Sinbad asks.

I pull my arm back down and feel some resistance to the motion. It doesn't stop the movement entirely; it just makes it sluggish. Taking it a step further, I attempt to walk around. My legs feel the same resistance as my arm did, and I move in short, jerking motions.

"Interesting," Sinbad remarks, "I can exert some influence on your body, but you seem to be ultimately in control."

On a hunch, I mentally ask him, *Can you hear me now?*

His usual voice echoes in my head. *Quite clearly, yes, I can. It would seem that, in this state, our connection goes very deep, indeed.*

Getting back to what you were saying, I think to him, *while I do remain in charge of my body, I think it's possible to hand over my control to you if I choose. I wonder if you could enter people uninvited and take control of their actions in a similar way?*

I've honestly no idea, Sinbad admits. *However, I can't imagine being inside someone who doesn't want me there, unless my need were rather dire.*

I understand. You're a good and kind person.

Am I? my ghostly passenger counters. *I've done many things in my life that were decidedly unkind and far from good.*

We all have our pasts.

I feel my throat being cleared as my hand scratches my collarbone nervously. It's a strange feeling—being inside my body with someone else at the helm.

It's then that I remember the feeling of Sinbad's hands when they passed over my breasts and the resulting tingle that ensued from deep within me. I wonder…

The smile on my lips is my own doing. *What if…* I start, then lose my nerve.

What if? Sinbad pushes.

What if I were to get undressed? You could… explore my body with my hands.

A jolt of panic runs through me at this unexpected offer. *Are you certain? I have no desire to do anything you think inappropriate.*

I can sense his reluctance to take full advantage of the situation and I'm reminded of how deeply he cares about me. I know he'd never harm me or cross any lines with which I'm uncomfortable. But, for now, I want him to explore me. I want to know what it feels like—what he feels like.

I want to touch you, Bowie, Sinbad says.

The familiar feelings his thoughts provoke make my chest grow tight, and the valley between my legs feels hot and damp. The sudden need for something carnal between the two of us attacks me with such vehemence, I have to brace myself to avoid falling on my knees. Somehow, I retain enough presence of mind to reply, *then touch me.*

I strip off my clothes by the light of my lantern and then glance down at myself, taking myself in from Sinbad's point of view. It's odd to feel so attracted to myself, so turned on by my erect nipples and the thatch of blonde hair between my legs.

May I touch you? he asks.

Yes.

This is all so strange for me. I'm looking at myself through our shared eyes, and his obvious appreciation for my form allows me to see myself in a different light, a better light. I normally view myself as short and scrawny—little. But I can sense Sinbad's impression of me, which is petite and beautiful. He expresses his love for my body with my own hands.

Your body is a marvel—every curve, every dip is pure beauty.

I feel my hands running down my breasts, pausing at each nipple to squeeze them slightly until the tips harden to rocks. He chuckles from within me as both of us are overcome with the feelings of my hands. Soon I feel myself reaching lower still.

You will tell me if I go too far? Sinbad asks.

Yes, I answer, though I know I won't stop him. And as the thought crosses my mind, I realize he knows it too.

This sensation of being both the giver and the receiver of pleasure is...

Incredible, I finish for him as my fingers part the thatch of hair and I feel my own wetness. He sighs contentedly, using my lungs and mouth.

I think I could exist inside you forever.

I finger the sensitive nub between my legs and throw my head back as I sigh, long and hard. I'm not sure whether it's Sinbad's response or mine. And it doesn't matter. All that does matter is the feeling of bliss that blossoms up within me as I deftly touch myself, my fingers moving lower to my opening.

I want to feel the inside of you, Sinbad whispers.

I can't respond other than to moan as he pushes one of my fingers into my opening. My channel is tight but slick and I can feel my own walls pushing against my finger.

You are so tight, so small, Sinbad says. *Have you ever had a man inside you?*

Never, I answer.

Oh, Bowie, you have no idea how I wish I could have been the first man to thrust inside you—to teach you what love is between a man and a woman.

I wish that too, Sinbad.

My hands don't feel like they're mine as I touch myself. Even so, I find myself wishing Sinbad had another body to possess, so that we could truly give ourselves to each another.

My fingers easily find my hard, pulsating clit as they pull out of my opening. He slowly strokes it back and forth, with a deliberate purpose. I moan and he responds by returning to the area of my wetness. He knows exactly what I feel when he slips one finger and then two into my hungry folds, massaging me in precisely the right spot.

My body quakes when Sinbad gives me an earth-shattering orgasm, the likes of which I've never managed to achieve on my own. He uses my hand like a true master, starting out so slow and light, before pushing harder and more deliberate. In seconds, my entire body explodes with a series of satisfying climaxes that spiral out from my core.

I'm dimly aware of my loud moaning each time I reach the precipice. For a moment, I wonder if the others can hear me. Then I decide I don't care if they can. Let them listen! This is so exquisite and I'm enjoying every single moment so much, I don't want it to end. It's unparalleled to anything I've experienced.

When my body can no longer take another orgasm, I collapse against the base of a tree and try to catch my breath.

Can you feel the same pleasure I did? I ask Sinbad.

Absolutely! And may I say that it's amazing? A woman's climax is so different to a man's.

How so?

A man's is very centralized and explosive. Yours begins in the same place, but the sensations you receive are so different... I shiver with his unbridled delight. *They spread throughout your body, tingling every inch of your skin, and sparking every one of your nerves. Your orgasm builds and grows inside you until it takes control of your entire body.*

You can feel all that? I ask him. *Did you receive that much pleasure from my climax too?*

To an extent, but I doubt it was complete, Sinbad admits. *I imagine what you felt was tremendously more powerful than the intense, but secondhand experience I received.*

I calmly stroke my still-hardened nipples, sending fresh shivers through my body. *I wish I could give you more.*

No need. What we just shared was amazing. For allowing me that experience, I thank you.

"Don't thank me for it," I say aloud, somewhat embarrassed by his unsolicited gratitude.

I have so much to be grateful for. You rescued me from the Mallow Fields, where I would have still been trying to figure out what happened to me.

And that's when Jack's ugly words about the disappearance of all the shepherds returns to me. *I just wish there were more of us. If something happens to me, there will be no shepherds left, and then I don't know what will happen.*

Do you think what Jack said could be the reason why are there no more shepherds? Sinbad asks. *Because it did make a lot of sense to me and if Jack is correct, you could well be in grave danger.*

104

After we return to my tent, I lay down upon my bed and we lie in silence for a while, both of us examining our own thoughts. My mind is stuck on the scarcity of shepherds and, of course, Jack's words. His theory goes way beyond mere coincidence or random misfortune. Why am I still alive while the others aren't? Is it simply because Morningstar hasn't found me yet? Or have I been spared for another reason?

All these questions with no answers frustrates me to no end. Nothing makes any sense anymore, not even death. With so much magic floating around, and the never ending struggle between good and evil, the Chosen Ones versus dark forces, I suppose it's small wonder why we're surrounded by chaos. Despite the prophecy, no one really knows what the future holds, not even, I daresay, Morningstar himself. Perhaps we have to let the destined events just happen and sort out everything afterwards.

Even as I try to find peace with that thought, I know I'm not being realistic. Whatever negative forces can be stopped from happening, should be stopped. That's why I'm here, and no matter how disgusted, frustrated and angry I might become with my companions, I'm bound to fulfill my purpose. I may fail in my effort to oppose the enemy, but I have to do everything within my power to prevent things from getting worse.

Sinbad, I ask, *do you think we're even capable of interceding with whatever the gods have in store for us?*

Perhaps Claude is a better person to ask that question?

I'm not sure I'll get the right answer from him.

I'm merely a simple sailor at heart, Bowie.

But you've seen many things that none of us have seen and I value your opinion. I take a breath and then continue. *If the gods decide our fates, isn't it wrong to oppose what they deem appropriate for us?*

Everything I've seen in life indicates that the gods are indifferent to our mortal existence. Mostly, they seem content to let us handle ourselves and our own problems.

But aren't they responsible for us since they created us… at least, according to legend?

True, but they don't control every aspect of our being. I think they provide us with the tools we need to make the most of our lives on earth.

I must accept that answer, I reply, though still unsatisfied with it. *I try to imagine all the dark magic and evil spells that threaten good, upstanding people—those who don't deserve so much pain and tragedy—and I have to wonder why the gods allow such inhumanity to exist.*

We all wonder why dreadful things happen, Bowie. The only certainty I know is that no one has the answers.

We continue to relax, contemplating our inner thoughts in silence. Then, after a while, Sinbad speaks with my voice. "Shall I leave you now?"

In that moment, I briefly wish we could just stay

here, like this, forever. But I know we can't. We can't defy the laws of nature. Yet, I don't want Sinbad to leave me.

"No, not yet," I say aloud. "Let's stay together a while longer."

I'll not argue. I love being here like this with you. There's a pause in his thought before he adds, *In truth, I think I love you.*

I love you too, I answer honestly.

The warm sensation arises again, tempting me to enjoy another round of self-stimulation. But instead, we just bask in our spiritual bond. I wonder what the others might think of us being combined in one body. Now, it doesn't seem the least bit unusual. Furthermore, there's no doubt in my mind that this won't be the last time we unite inside my body. As long as we both remain in the same realm, I plan to enjoy this newfound ability as often as I can.

Chapter Ten
Jack
A Week Later

As we train, I have to tear my eyes away from Bowie.

Since we arrived at the front, our sessions have put us very close to one another, maybe too close. I've noticed in the last few days that my thoughts of her are nonstop—ever since I witnessed the raw power flowing through her. But my thoughts aren't just about her abilities—they're about her, period. The way she moves, the way she speaks, the look in her eyes, the fact that she can't stand me.

I regret that fact the most.

I was too harsh with her earlier and now I'm paying for that misstep. She looks at Claude with all the kindness in the world and I can tell she has a close connection with the spirit. She regards Dolion with a detached sort of respect, but I can see her desire for him in the depths of her eyes. I'm the only one she can't seem to stand and I have myself to thank.

I don't understand this blossoming need I have to correct things between us, but regardless, it's there. I wish she would look at me the way she looks at Claude. And, even though I've done what I can to correct the ugliness between us, nothing seems to be working.

Lately, I've been doing lots of thinking about love. No, I'm not in love with her—obviously, I barely even know her. But the more general subject of love has been visiting me with more regularity than it used to. And love is something I can ill afford. It's a state of being I swore off years ago because I fear it makes me weak, vulnerable.

So, love is off the table here—it's not something I will even allow myself to travel near. No, I will continue to keep my eye on the prize, as it were. To continue to shun all other avenues of my life because we have a mission to accomplish. And how we accomplish that mission could make all the difference in the world as to whether or not we prevail in this war.

The more of Morningstar's army of men we can clear out, the easier it will be to battle Morningstar, himself. But time is rapidly dwindling and we're quickly approaching the last moments of our preparation. We can't afford any mistakes.

"Are you ready?" I ask Bowie as we square off against one another in the clearing. We each hold magicked swords that cut through the air with blades made of light energy, pulled from the very ether around us. The blades disable any real damage from being done, should we accidentally hit one another.

But Bowie can't rely solely on her magical powers, as she might not be capable of accessing them at times. The ceaseless threat of an ambush could also engage us, which would leave her in a vulnerable situation. That's why she must master all weapons: spears, swords, daggers, and maces. Her extraordinary powers are an undeniable asset, but they only go so far in battle, where the enemy's magic could be far more powerful than hers.

She raises her sword and nods. "I am."

Without another word, I lunge forward. She parries, thrusting her sword at me, and we begin clashing blade to blade—hers blue energy and mine green. Pops of electricity fizzle in the air each time we make contact.

Immediately, I can feel the fact that her power has grown. She turns her small stature into a strategic asset. Her increased flexibility shines as she thrusts and deflects my attack. Some of the timidity I witnessed when we first began our training, over two weeks ago, is still in place, but it's nothing compared to what it was. I'm fairly sure she's fully accepted the fact that she is one of the Chosen and, therefore, has her own part to play in saving Fantasia.

Now to hone her skills to a razor's edge.

We move back and forth like ballet dancers, fully engaged in our mock battle. She suddenly rushes me, forcing me to retreat and as I do so, the back of my left foot encounters a fallen tree. Immediately, I lose my balance and fall backwards over the felled tree, my blade going to one side as I tumble.

As soon as I land (on my ass), I'm overcome by a fit of laughter as I think about how ridiculous this scene must appear: me, a seasoned warrior, being bested by a tiny shepherdess! Before this conflict is over, I predict she'll be my greatest protégé.

She smiles in triumph as she holds the tip of her sword against my throat. "Do you surrender unconditionally?"

It seems the ugliness between us is forgotten, at least for the moment.

My laughter diminishes to a chuckle. "This one time, I do." She withdraws her blade and lets me rise to my feet. I notice she doesn't offer me a hand up and I can't help but imagine such wouldn't be the same were I Claude, maybe even Dolion.

Without my blade, I still immediately attack her. I can't let her relax for a single moment. No battle is easy.

"I'm tired!" she calls out as she jumps aside, barely missing my attempt to bulldoze her to the ground.

I reach for my sword and grabbing it, deftly turn on my toes and thrust it forward, aiming for her midsection, a blow which she deftly dodges. "The enemy doesn't take breaks! That's why it's important to build up your stamina; you have to keep fighting longer than any of them can."

She thrusts her sword at my arm, which I deflect. "But I caught you last time," she points out. "No reason to pursue a fight *after* I've already killed you."

"You never have just one enemy on the field of battle," I say. "Replacements keep coming..." I jab my blade at her face, but she smoothly ducks the move. "And they don't retreat…" I sweep at her legs, but she avoids the blow just in time. "… Until one of you expires." My overhand strike towards her brow is successfully blocked.

"I thought Dolion wanted me to use my powers to reap the souls of all our foes," she says while perfectly executing a number of thrusts I'm ashamed to admit I struggle to deflect.

"You must be prepared for anything," I tell her. "The strain of using your powers will weaken you."

"I didn't seem very weak when I scorched that clearing," she argues.

I shake my head. "Things won't always be like that time in the clearing. You'll be taking hundreds—maybe even thousands—of lives all at once. Eventually, you'll recover from that enormous drain, but you have to be able to defend yourself during your weakest moments."

Again, our blades clash until she finally falters. At her moment of weakness, I pounce on her, pushing her to the ground and pinning her there. It's only then that I realize how stricken her expression is.

She's scared of me.

I can see the truth of as much in her eyes— how wide they are. Proof is also in the way she swallows hard, and her breathing hitches. I don't want her to be afraid of me, so I jump up immediately.

"Do you surrender unconditionally?" I ask, smiling broadly and using my most reassuring tone.

"I do," she replies, her worry swiftly replaced by relief.

My original goal was to scare her, but I regret that now. Of course, she'll face much worse combat on the battlefield, but she isn't a natural warrior, born to slaughter men by the bushel. She's a Chosen One solely because of her magical skills, not her prowess in warfare.

This can't be easy for her, I tell myself. *And the fact that she's come this far is proof of her incredible courage. Courage you mocked the first time you sparred.*

"Bowie," I say without even realizing the words leave my lips.

She looks up at me expectantly, the energy magic of her blade disappearing into her hand.

"Yes?"

And though I feel the words on the edge of my tongue, it's as though I'm suddenly paralyzed—I can't bring myself to say them.

"Are we done for the day?" she asks, her expression seemingly disappointed.

"Yes," I say quickly and, as she turns around, the rest of the words birth themselves from my lips. "I'm sorry about what I said."

She turns around to face me. "What you said?"

"In the clearing," I explain. "When I called you a coward." I clear my throat and feel the guilt cresting within me. "I didn't mean it. You... you have much more courage than I gave you credit for."

She smiles slightly. "Thank you."

"You're welcome," I answer and suddenly have to resist the urge to reach out and grip her, pulling her into my arms so I can hold her tightly. But I don't do anything. I just stand there, all the while losing myself in the deep blue of her eyes.

"I appreciate you saying that, Jack," she says as she takes a few steps closer to me.

And before I realize what I'm doing, I close the distance that separates us and reach out, caressing my index finger down her cheek. She doesn't pull away, which surprises me. She just stands there, within arm's reach, and looks up at me while I look down at her.

"I've treated you atrociously," I start, my voice deep and almost caught in my throat. "And I... I feel very guilty and ashamed."

"Jack," she says and her tone is soft, hypnotic almost. Before I realize what I'm doing, I lower my head and she raises hers and I can tell I'm going to kiss her.

All at once, whatever moment is currently unraveling between us is suddenly shattered by the unexpected appearance of Dolion.

"I assigned you the job of preparing Bowie for battle and instead, I discover you taking liberties with her," Dolion announces as he pulls out his sword and parks it under my chin. "I should end you right here and now," he growls at me with deadly solemnity.

I'm completely shocked by his response. I didn't imagine Dolion one for jealousy and though he's looked at Bowie with the same desire as Claude and me, he's never made it known that his interests were anything more than carnal where she was concerned, nor that he would ever act on them.

"He didn't take any liberties with me!" Bowie protests as she backs away from me and pushes the blade away from my neck. As she looks at him, her eyes narrow and fire burns their depths.

Dolion looks at her. "Don't defend him."

She continues to glare at him. "And what difference does it make to you if he did make advances on me?" she replies defiantly and I can't help my surprise—I never thought in a million years she would defend me.

For a moment, Dolion just stands there, saying nothing. Then he calmly sheathes his sword. "Perhaps I overreacted," he says. Then he sticks a long finger in my face. "But *you* should know better than to put yourself in such a compromising position." He takes a breath. "We are here to protect her, not to bed her."

Chapter Eleven
Bowie

"Let me talk to Dolion," I tell Jack, putting my hand on his chest.

He shakes his head and says, "Don't jeopardize your own reputation by trying to save mine."

"Never mind my reputation," I say, as I leave Jack in search of Dolion. Whatever harsh words Dolion had for Jack, they weren't warranted. In fact, I was and still am surprised by Dolion's reaction—he seemed so angry.

As soon as I see Dolion, I call out to him. He doesn't even glance over his shoulder, but keeps walking. I grip his arm and stop him, "Dammit, Dolion, stop!"

For a moment, I expect him to strike me for getting in his way. I brace myself for the impact, but it never comes. After waiting several silent moments, I say, "Let's talk about this."

"Talk about what?" he snaps. "You teasing all the men in this camp? Knowing you can

117

seduce anyone you want and finding power in it?"

His words burn me with their scalding anger, and his own anger is infectious. My palm slaps his cheek loudly, and I'm actually proud of the satisfying sound it makes. He has no right to speak to me that way.

"You will speak to me with the respect I'm due," I demand.

"Respect?" he laughs, shaking his head before his eyes narrow. "How many of us are you bedding? Am I the only one left out in the cold?"

I further glare at him. "I'm bedding no one, though it's none of your goddamned business." I see a small twinge of hurt in his eyes, so I press on. "What's it to you, anyway? I don't owe you or anyone else here a single thing."

"While that is true, it seems Jack was getting something for free," he spits.

The next slap I attempt fails to hit the mark. He grabs my wrist before I make contact. "I will not have you continue to play games with my men."

"I'm not playing games with any of them," I reply defensively.

He throws my hand aside. "And if you weren't so busy sashaying your feminine lures about, perhaps we'd see more progress in your training."

His audacious comment makes everything much clearer. "Jealousy doesn't become you, commander," I sneer.

"I am hardly jealous," he laughs without mirth.

"While that is certainly debatable, of one thing I want to make abundantly clear: you have no claim on me. No one owns me, least of all, you."

"I don't argue that."

"Then *what* are you arguing?"

He inhales deeply. "I don't want you messing with the men's heads—not when we are this close to battle."

"Duly noted," I spit the words back at him.

As I turn to retreat, he reaches out and grips my wrist and then something happens that I struggle to describe. It's as if a screen drops behind my eyelids and projected upon the screen are visions and images of another life, another time.

I can see Dolion with a woman and the woman with him is someone who means everything to him. I can feel as much in the expression of love in his eyes. Though I can't see the woman's face or features, I can see her lithe body and the way she dances round him, teasing him, and he laughs as he reaches out for her. But she's just out of his grasp, laughing and dancing as if she doesn't have a care in the world.

The vision only lasts for a second, and Dolion drops his hold of my wrist. I can't tell whether he's aware of what just passed between us, but I'm panting from the shock. "I *saw* her," I say as he looks at me with confusion in his eyes.

"You saw who?"

"A woman," I answer. "A woman you loved," I explain. "She was the only woman you ever loved," I continue, not even sure where the words are coming from, but they're dropping from my lips and there's nothing I can do to stop them. "Now and *always*."

He steps toward me with a look of pure anguish on his face. His nose is barely one inch from mine when he speaks again. "I don't know what you think you saw."

"I saw it as soon as you touched me."

He breathes in deeply, but then shrugs away the concern in my eyes. "It doesn't matter; she's dead anyway."

"What?"

I'm surprised to hear him admit this woman is real—that what I just saw is true and valid. Yet, he seems unable to lie—at least in this moment.

"Who is she?" I ask.

He won't meet my gaze. "She's dead. I lost her as a result of this war."

"I'm sorry," I breathe.

He nods and insists on staring at the ground beneath us.

"You loved her," I say.

He nods again. "I loved her with all my heart when she was alive. And I still love her now. I've never stopped. It's taken…" His throat needs clearing before he can continue. "It's taken me a long time to realize love doesn't magically disappear after someone stops breathing. It'd be so much easier if it did."

"I'm… sorry, Dolion," I whisper.

He clears his throat again, and tries to restrain his grief before he continues. "Time is healing my wounds, be it ever so slowly," he says. Then he grows quiet as he looks at something past me, in the distance—it's as though he's looking at something from his past. "I thought I would never get beyond my feelings for her," he continues and then his eyes land on mine. "Until I met you."

"Me?"

He nods and his eyes are deep, penetrating as they search mine. "But I'm mistaken in my hasty assumption and unfathomable hope that you might feel something for me, too."

His confession leaves me speechless and I don't know what to do or say. I just stand there, looking up at him with what be a completely dumbfounded expression.

"Tell me you feel something for me?" he asks.

I search my mind and my heart, trying to understand what I feel for him. Whatever it is, it's complicated. It's not easy to trust him and feel close to him as it is with Claude. And with Jack—it seems we, too, have forgiven one another for things we said in the past. And, of course, my feelings for Dolion can't compare with my feelings for Sinbad. Yet, I...

"I do feel something for you," I manage.

I'm still contemplating what I think, and feel, and need to say when he suddenly grabs me and pulls me closer to him. For a moment, I want to flee, but before I can think another thought, he covers my mouth with his in a tender, but passionate kiss. And all my thoughts of angst, anger and distrust seem to completely exit my mind. It's as if whatever thoughts were previously there are gone, wiped out. Now my mind is just a vacant lot.

All I can think of, all I can focus on is Dolion.

It's odd because I've never felt this way about him before—as if he's the answer to my everything.

This isn't right, Bowie, my voice sounds in my head. *Where is Sinbad?*

Something frantic starts to build within me as I try to reach out to my friend, the one person who is always near me, day and night. Yet I can't feel Sinbad and I can't see him and that isn't right, not with the tether between us.

Nevermind that, another voice sounds in my thoughts. *Focus on the here and now, on Dolion.*

My head grows cloudy as Dolion takes my hand and leads me inside his tent. My head is still spinning from his kiss and as soon as the clouds begin to dissipate, he kisses me again. All of a sudden, it's as if I can't see straight, can't think, can't even talk.

Instead, I'm vaguely aware of him slowing undressing me as my traitorous body allows him to continue. As he nuzzles my bare skin with his mouth, his lips plant the softest kisses on my neck as though he's marking a trail.

Somewhere, deep in the back of my mind, a voice yells at me to stop, to think about what I'm doing and to wake up from this oblivion that's overtaken my mind, but I can't seem to fight the flow of contentedness that washes over me. It's like trying to swim upstream in a raging current. I simply can't do it.

"You are extraordinarily beautiful," Dolion murmurs as he drops to his knees in front of me. When I glance down at myself, I realize I'm completely naked. I don't even remember him taking my clothes off.

"I don't…"

"Shh," he says as he grips my rear in each hand and pulls me into his face. His tongue slips between my folds and before I can understand what's happening, I feel him lapping at me, licking circles around my clit and sucking on it as blissful feelings start to blossom within my core.

The cloudiness in my mind continues to expand until I'm not even aware of thinking anything any longer. There's only the feel of Dolion's tongue on my sensitive nub and then his fingers replacing his tongue as they delve down towards my entrance. He pushes my legs apart and slips a finger inside me as I throw my head back and moan.

"That's it," he says, encouraged by the wetness spreading between my legs. "Tell me you are mine."

"I'm," I start and buck against him as he thrusts another finger inside me, pushing in and out.

"Say it."

"I'm yours," I whisper. Somehow, the words sound foreign on my tongue—wrong, but I can't fight them.

His mouth covers mine in a lingering kiss and he tangles one hand in my hair, softly kneading my right breast with the other. When his thumb slightly pinches my nipple, ripples of delight undulate through me.

124

My hips buck against him, inviting him to do more, and letting him know how eager I am. He moves his fingers back down to the valley between my thighs and begins to play my sensitive nub as if he's manipulating an orchestra.

Despite my urgency, he takes maddeningly slow strokes and teases my clit until it swells like a balloon and throbs with desire. He persists in his sensuous torture, keeping me on the verge of a climax before easing off and letting my pleasure ebb. Then he starts it all over again, climbing the crescendo with renewed vigor. My pleasure is even more magnified each time he denies me a climax; and every time I ascend the precipice, it's an agonizing, but satisfying exercise.

Just when I can't take anymore, he pulls away. I groan in despair when he stands up and looks down at me. "What are you doing?" I breathlessly inquire.

"Giving you what you want," he replies, quickly removing his clothes until he joins me in my nakedness. His body is impressive, tall and sinewy. Like any successful warrior, he's muscular and scarred from battle. Of course, right now, his most noticeable appendage is the sizable erection swinging between his legs.

I turn away in a moment of modesty. Despite my willingness now, I've yet to surrender my virginity to any man. I've never seen a naked man, never mind an aroused and naked man, and though I find Dolion fascinating, I'm also very unsure of myself.

"What's wrong?" he asks, kneeling down and caressing my cheek.

"Nothing… I'm just… I've never been with a man."

His head jerks up in surprise. "What about the others?"

"No!" I repeat, insisting that I'm telling the truth.

He slips two fingers inside me, as if he seeks the proof of my words. He breaks into a broad smile. "Then I shall make you mine." He pulls me towards him and gives me another kiss. "And mine you will remain." He looks at me then and holds my gaze. "I don't share my women."

"Oh, okay," I say, somewhat taken aback.

"And once I give you my seed, you will be mine, Bowie."

My head swirls with happy thoughts, thoughts that are fresh and new to me but also as old as time itself.

This is right. This is true. This is what was meant to happen, that strange voice echoes through my mind.

But, I start to fight it and another cloud of confusion dizzies my mind. *Sinbad, Claude and*

Jack…

Your flirtation with Jack and the spiritual union you shared with Sinbad don't compare to this. The desire and comradery you have with Claude doesn't compare to this.

When Dolion touches me and holds me, something happens that I've never experienced before—feelings of complete bliss.

Yet, that voice still yells at me. That voice that's so far away—as if at the end of a very long tunnel. It screams that something isn't right, that I need to wake up and see the truth.

But I can't focus on it long. Not when Dolion lowers me to the cot, then climbs atop me and positions himself to enter me for the first time. He deliberately moves very slowly, pushing his tip gradually into my wet folds while he kisses and holds me, nearly bisecting me with his considerable girth. It doesn't hurt, which surprises me. I was always told the first time is the worst time.

I welcome the tears, letting the proof of my happiness roll down my face as Dolion impales my maidenhead for the first time. Perhaps he's right when he says I'm his now. Maybe we do belong to one another.

Our bodies move in perfect rhythm, bringing me ever closer to that sweet, blessed edge. However, Dolion doesn't tease me or try to enhance the suspense. He pushes me right over the cliff. I dig my fingers deep into his back, holding on as I convulse helplessly from my descent into orgasm. My entire being explodes from within, sending shockwaves that vibrate every fiber of my body.

"Good girl," he groans before releasing his own climax. I feel it pulsing in my center, filling me with his warmth. "You are fully mine now."

Everything washes over and through me at once, the heat of the moment culminating into what I know to be true.

Dolion loves me! And I love him too.

Chapter Twelve
Bowie
Two Weeks Later

"Are you ready for this, Bowie?" Dolion asks me as we approach the enemy camp on horseback in the late afternoon.

"I think so," I reply.

The truth is, I'm terrified. I can't imagine how I'll pull this off. I've practiced using my powers against the false fronts Jack sets up. But that's very different from what I'll encounter once we hit the actual camps.

The idea that I have to reap so many souls at once leaves me afraid and riddled with guilt. I still wonder if I possess that much power, although Jack assures me I do. Actually, my power seems to have grown stronger the longer I've been in the company of these three men. Whether it's due to Jack and his training or something else, I can't be certain. Even with all of that, though, I wonder, will it be enough? We don't even know how many men are stationed at each of the camps. They constantly migrate

129

from one camp to the next, preparing for battle and shifting periodically so we don't know what to expect.

"Don't *think so*," Jack admonishes me, "*know so*. Be ready for this."

There haven't been many words between Jack and me since Dolion claimed me as his own. It seems that since then, I haven't spent much time without Dolion. Whenever I find myself alone with either Jack or Claude, Dolion seems to suddenly appear. It's almost as if he doesn't like the idea of me being alone with either of them.

And Sinbad—he's been uncharacteristically quiet, as well. It seems as though every time I seek his council, he isn't there. And when he is there, Dolion is quick to also appear. Needless to say, Sinbad and I haven't shared another of our moments of possession since Dolion claimed me. And, most recently, our tether has felt off somehow—as if it isn't as strong now as it was before. I used to be able to feel Sinbad— almost as if he were part of me and now I can't.

"Then yes, I'm ready," I tell Jack. "Physically and magically."

At the sound of twigs breaking beneath heavy bootfalls, I look over and see Dolion. He smiles at me and that same cloud of confusion settles into my mind. It's as though every time I see him, I'm overcome by the love between us.

I lose my train of thought and my focus, and all I can see is him.

"Very good," Dolion says approvingly. "You will need both before this is over."

"Do we know how many men there are in the camps?" I ask, fighting to stay on topic.

"Wish we did," Claude says as he walks up beside Dolion. "We'll do some quick reconnaissance to see what we can learn."

"Only if we have the time to find out before they spot us," Dolion adds in frustration.

I nod and remain silent, steeling my nerves for what's to come. Jack has done all he can to train me. But as he's so fond of repeating, our training is nothing compared to what we'll face in actual battle. I may be a Chosen One, but I can't be cocky or stupid about this.

As soon as we pass the next copse of trees, Claude whispers, "We're here."

My heart skips a beat. I thought it would take longer to reach our destination. And as I face my fate now, I fear I'm going to pass out.

Sinbad speaks quietly in my ear. "Just relax, Bowie. You can do this."

I brace myself and respond, "I have to untether you and let you roam free for a bit, just like in the Mallow Fields."

"Why?" he asks curiously.

"Because if I don't, there's a good chance you'll be reaped with the rest of the souls I must harvest now."

I feel the distinctive feathery brush of his ghostly hand on my cheek. "This world doesn't deserve you, Bowie. Small wonder why I love you."

As much as I can, I lean into his touch. "I love you too, Sinbad." The words feel foreign on my tongue, but true. A second later, I'm overcome with guilt as I imagine Dolion's face and the love we share. If I love Dolion, how can I love another man?

It's a question I can't afford to ponder.

After I cut the ties between Sinbad and myself, I mourn the loss of that connection. "And I promise this much," I say to mask my sorrow, "I *will* get you where you belong after this is over."

As he drifts away, Sinbad asks, "And what if my true place is by your side?"

Before I can respond, he's already gone. I sincerely hope he's as far from the camp as possible.

"It's time," Jack says, and his grim announcement banishes my thoughts of Sinbad.

I turn to face forward and in the distance, I can just manage to make out the camp through the thick vale of trees.

Dolion points up to a bluff that overlooks the camp. "Up there," he says. "That should give us the view we need."

After tying off the horses near some wild rye for them to graze on, we go up the slight incline to observe the camp below. Even from this far away, the camp is humming and bustling with activity. The camp is a large one and extends as far as we can see, tent after tent forming a long perimeter. The rear section is protected by an old fortress wall. How many men are currently residing there? It's nearly impossible to know. But there are many, many more than the four of us.

Dolion takes all this in with his usual stoicism. "Bowie, the moment we arrive, you'll have to take out as many as you can."

"Wasn't that always the plan?" I quip.

"I'm serious," Dolion counters. "They'll be on the attack as soon as they spot us. Taking down as many as you can get in one swipe will determine if we have a fighting chance against the rest."

I nod, doing my best to conceal my panic. How many must I take at one strike? How quickly will we be killed if I don't take out enough of them?

"Should we wait until first light?" Jack asks. "They may be a little less active the closer it gets to dawn."

"No, we can't risk it," Dolion says. "The element of surprise is on our side right now. The alerts run from sunset to sunrise. They'll never see us coming in broad daylight."

"Also, the longer we sit here," Claude interjects, "the better our chances of being discovered. If that happens, we don't have a prayer in all the nine hells."

"Then what are we waiting for?" I say, eager for our first victory. However misplaced my confidence might be, I cast any doubts clean out of my mind. Victories are not won but manifested; you must first believe in them before you can see them. War is as much about having a proper mindset as it is the proper skills. Or, at least, that's what Jack keeps going on and on about.

We move quietly through the trees, a tiny raiding party silently descending on the camp. I can hear the men engaging in their own training when we arrive, the mock struggles make them oblivious to the real enemy, waiting just outside their gates. There are only a handful of men on guard, not enough to pose a problem if anything goes sour.

Above them flies a flag of black with gold etching around the corners and gold threaded within the middle. It's the insignia of Morningstar and seeing the flag flying proudly in the air now—it bolsters me and gives me confidence that what I'm about to do is for the benefit of Fantasia.

Dolion motions for me to take the lead, and I do. Any minute now, despite our adequate cover, we'll be spotted. There's just too much daylight for us not to be noticed.

It's time.

I direct my attention to the men at the front, both the guards at the gates and those who are training behind them. A surge of energy rushes upward through my body, moving into a shockwave of power. A bright light fills the air around me before pulsating outward and blasting towards the camp.

One of the guards sees me, his eyes growing wide just as the massive wave hits him. The blast sends him and his fellow guards spiraling backwards off their feet, tossing them like dead leaves onto the ground. Briefly, their screams can be heard before they drop off and their souls are snapped away in a flash of white light. Nothing but empty vessels are left behind.

Behind them, the wave sweeps through the rest of the men. I watch them drop like flies, their souls rising into the air as they take their last breaths. The air is teeming with their spirits—temporarily lost and without any understanding of what just happened to them. I push out another wave that elevates their souls into the ether for the time being. Many of them will wander there until they find the afterlife on their own. Others will need my guidance.

I can feel the expense of my energy. My shoulders sag and I try not to fall to my knees. It's due to much more than just the energy I've expended though—it's something deeper, something that will now be forever etched in my blood. Guilt.

The guilt haunts me and I can't imagine it will ever let up—even though this is the right thing to be doing and we're only helping our own side by destroying these evil men, I can't help but feel as if what I've done is wrong.

Strangely, I'm not so much heartbroken about taking their lives as I am about not escorting them to the otherworld. By rights, I should be ferrying their souls to their rightful afterlives as we speak. Yet here I am, unable to move—drained to the point of exhaustion. No sooner do I think that thought than the remainder of the camp discovers something has happened.

"We're under attack!" someone cries just before the survivors surge across their dead comrades to assail us.

I panic.

The initial wave of my strike takes a lot more out of me than I expected. Escorting so many souls across the threshold at once will require even more time for me to recover. Yet I can't move, and I can't think clearly.

I glance down and notice a sullied piece of a flag sticking out from underneath a pile of rubble. I reach for it and pulling it up, realize it's a piece of a flag but it's not the flag I saw flying overhead earlier. This flag is blue with red piping and it bears the insignia of the Guild.

"No," I say and inhale deeply as I pull the tattered flag to my chest.

I'm dimly aware of an arrow sailing past my head before Claude scoops me up and drapes me over his shoulder like a sack of flour before he starts running.

"Claude, it's a Guild flag!" I say to him as he rushes me to safety. "This wasn't Morningstar's camp! It was one of our own!"

From my off-kilter vantage point, I can see Dolion and Jack heading back into the forest. What are they doing? This isn't what we planned. Why are we retreating from the fight?

It seems like forever as we hurry through the woods. And I must assume the men from the camp are probably close on our heels. My heart starts to race, which thankfully clears the fog from my head.

When we finally stop running, I realize I must have blacked out because I find myself inside a cabin I don't remember ever entering.

Claude helps me to a seat beside a wooden table and drops down to his haunches as he studies me. We spend a moment just looking at one another as if we can't believe what just happened.

Chapter Thirteen
Claude

Once we're inside the cabin and out of harm's reach, I sit Bowie down. "This will have to do for a bit," I tell her.

"Claude, this flag," she says as she hands me the remains of what was once a Guild flag. I take it from her, but shake my head.

"It means nothing," I say. "It was Morningstar's camp—you saw the flag before we attacked."

She nods, but there's confusion in her gaze. "Then how do you explain that?" she says and points to the blue fabric in my hand.

"Morningstar could have stolen it from one of the camps. For all we know, they could have been using it for target practice."

She swallows hard but appears to accept the reasoning in my response. "You need to relax and heal your magic, Bowie," I say.

She shakes her head. "I need… I need to return to make sure Sinbad is alright."

"He's a spirit," Dolion answers. "The time

to worry about whether he's alright is long past."

I turn to face him and give him an unencouraging glance before I return my attention to Bowie. "As Sinbad is tethered to you, you can feel him, no?"

She looks at me and nods. "I had to break the tether between us so I wouldn't accidentally reap him, but…" Her voice trails as she closes her eyes. "Yes, I… I can still feel him."

"Then he's fine, Bowie," I answer. "And I imagine it will simply be a matter of time before you're reunited."

"If you can feel your connection to Sinbad, can't he feel his connection to you?" Jack asks as he appears last in the doorway of the cabin and closes it behind him. Bowie looks at him and nods.

"Then he will come when he comes," I finish, and she looks at me with a slight smile. That's when she seems to take notice of her surroundings.

"Where are we?" she asks in a vacant voice.

"Just an old cabin, a fair distance from the camp," I answer.

I feel somewhat reassured when her eyes flicker with a little more life. At the sound of Jack bolting the door behind us, I feel slightly more reassured. Dolion, meanwhile, wastes

little time in lighting the nearest hanging wall
lantern so we can see.

"We need to scout the perimeter—make
sure we weren't followed here," Jack says as he
faces Dolion, who nods.

Dolion looks at me. "You stay here with
Bowie and see to it that she eats something."

I nod as I look to Jack, who says, "We'll be
back as soon as we do some reconnaissance."

Dolion approaches Bowie, who looks up at
him with a weary smile. I don't know what it is,
but there's something different about her—
whenever she's around Dolion, it's as if her
eyes glass over and her thinking clouds. Perhaps
it's just the makings of love? I'm unsure, but
there doesn't appear to be a change in Dolion—
he's just as dogmatic and rigid as he always
was.

"You did well out there, Bowie," he says in
that stiff manner of his. Then he leans down to
his haunches and takes her hand. "But you'll
need to do better."

She swallows hard and simply nods,
watching him as he stands and then approaches
Jack, who waits for him beside the door. They
unlatch it and then, moments later, Bowie and I
are alone.

"I believe what Dolion meant to say is you
were magnificent back there," I say, angry with
him for his choice of words.

Bowie's dreamy eyes drift towards the windows and it's as though my words are lost to her. "What if someone sees the lights within this place? Or follows us here? I'm not sure I'm..." Her exhaustion keeps her from talking for a moment before she tries again. "I'm not strong enough to fight them off yet."

"No one will know we're here." It's mostly the truth—anyone who followed us will simply have watched us vanish into seemingly nothing. But the truth of the matter is that the old cabin is magicked—it's one of many stopping points within Fantasia—stopping points meant to provide safe haven to those in support of the Guild. I nod toward the windows and door. "There are magical seals on all the windows and doors that prevent any light from escaping. Plus, an enchantment keeps this place invisible to others not in support of our cause. We will be safe here long enough for you to rest and regain your strength."

She shakes her head, the fogginess dulling the fear she's trying to explore. "They can still hear us, though."

"You think a place that conceals light would not do the same with noise?" I ask, even though I'm silently impressed she even considers all the potential issues of our newest location. "Per the spell, nothing leaves here unless it's purposely released."

142

"We're trapped in here?"

"No, nothing as worrisome as that," I tell her, cursing myself for my poor choice of words. "We can leave anytime we like." I help her up and she leans against me as I move her towards the only bed which occupies a far corner of the room.

"Lie down, Bowie," I tell her before I gently push her down when it seems she will argue with me. "And calm your thoughts. Relax."

At first, I think she's gasping from panic. Then I realize she's sobbing. "I don't know if I can, Claude," she tells me as her breathing becomes more ragged. "Those people… all those people… and so many screams. They were absolutely terrified as they died."

"They are the enemy." My voice sounds hollow to my own ears because I share in the shock she does. I wasn't prepared for the magnitude of her actions, even though I knew what to expect.

"They're still people."

"Bad people, Bowie." It's almost as though I'm attempting to convince myself as much as I am her.

Anger surges through her like an exploding volcano as she shakes her head and there appears to be confusion in her gaze. She just stares up at me for a moment or two. "I don't

143

know what I've done."

"You did what you had to do to progress our side, Bowie," I answer in a soft voice. "You have helped the Guild and Fantasia more than you could know."

"Those men believed as much in their own cause as we do in ours," she answers as she shakes her head.

I nod. "I don't know if I can give you the right answer, but what I do know is this: sometimes people think they're doing the right thing, but they really aren't. And none of their false righteousness can shield them when death finally claims them."

"How do we know we're not making the same mistake?"

"Rest now, Bowie. I'll make us something to eat."

"I'm not hungry, Claude," she says. "And I'm not tired."

Regardless, I walk into the small kitchen and grab a pair of tin plates from the cabinet at my feet. Then I pull out food from the storage cabinet above. Courtesy of the cabin's magic, I pull out a leg of roast chicken, a small cup of peas and two fresh carrots, which I put on her tin plate.

After doing the same for myself, I fetch a couple of tankards from the cabinet, both already filled with wine. I'm intoxicated by the strong scent of the wine. It'll help Bowie relax, possibly long enough to sleep once she has some food inside her. After that immense showing earlier, she'll need to eat and rest in order to rebuild her energy. Picking up our plates, I walk over to the bed and place one in front of her. She looks down at the food in surprise.

"How is this already prepared?"

"This place was built of magic and magic sustains it," I answer on a shrug before returning for her tankard and my own. I also snag two forks from the bottom cabinet and give one to her. She glances down at the food on her plate for barely half a second before picking up her fork. Once I'm seated, I do the same.

I'm pleased we came here. That first wave took much more out of Bowie than any of us expected, even Jack. Without her powers, we would have been grossly outmatched. Still, she did more damage in those first few moments than hundreds of men could have done in hours of fighting. That gives us a partial victory in my eyes.

But there appears no victory in Bowie's haunted expression. The distant look on her face is tainted by guilt. "Do you wish to talk about it?" I ask her gently.

"I just can't stop thinking about all those souls," she says, swallowing a mouthful of peas.

"I should be ferrying them across the threshold right now and, yet, here I am."

"Perhaps you'll get a chance to do so when this is over," I say. "For now, though, you can't dwell on those souls, Bowie. You're no good to anyone, not even yourself, if you don't eat and rest."

She frowns, but the color begins to return to her face. She eats more of her food, taking swigs of the wine between chewing. After a few moments, it's more than obvious that the food improves her health and outlook. She still seems drained, but she's more alert and aware than she was before. She finishes the last of her carrots and asks, "Do you think I'm an awful person for what I did today?"

"What? No!" I answer. "Of course, you aren't an awful person. If anything, you're the exact opposite: incredibly kind, good and caring."

She looks at her empty plate and then at the floor. "I don't feel very kind right now. All those screaming souls haunt me, Claude, and I don't imagine I'll ever be able to push their faces from my mind."

"They serve Morningstar."

"They are still people!" she exclaims, and I'm surprised by her anger. In a quieter, but no less agonized voice, she adds, "What I did today goes against everything I was ever taught. I shortened lives before they were meant to end. How do I live with that on my conscience?"

"It's never easy," I admit, "because you *have* a conscience. Battle affects everyone. The hardest part is living with yourself afterwards." I stretch my hand across the bed and lace my fingers with hers. "But I firmly believe all of us are worthy and can rise above the worst things we've done. And you are even more worthy."

She lifts her eyes to meet mine. "Do you really believe that?"

"With all my heart."

We say nothing for a few moments, but continue holding each other's hands and looking into each other's eyes. Using her free hand, she pushes her plate away. "I think I'll lie down now."

"I will sit by your bedside while you rest."

She nods and I return to the food in my lap. While I'm only half finished eating, I'm already satiated. I pick up both of our plates and return them to the upper cabinet.

My action doesn't go unnoticed. "You're just going to put the leftover food back?" Bowie grouses, wrinkling her nose as I close the cabinet door.

I smile and shake my head. "The cabin will take care of everything. Another of its delightful, little mysteries."

She closes her eyes and my heart goes out

to her. Between her words and sleepy expression, she looks so young. I find myself asking what distinguishes her as a Chosen One?

With her occupying the bed, I look for another place to lie down because I, too, am exhausted.

"Would you lie down next to me, Claude?" she asks in a half-conscious voice. "I don't really want to be alone right now."

"I, um…" I stammer, knowing Dolion won't like it if he sees us together in such close proximity. Of course, who knows how long he'll be gone. And once Bowie falls asleep, I can separate myself from her.

But do you trust yourself so close to her, Claude? I think.

While I'm just as attracted to her as I ever was, I do trust myself because I will always have her best interests first in my heart.

She holds her arms out like an eager bride craving the embrace of her new husband. "Please?"

I climb into bed with her, telling myself countless self-serving lies about being in such intimate quarters with this beauty. It's all innocent enough, I suppose. At least, that's what I hope.

"Men don't share their women."

It's a strange thing for her to say and I wonder why she'd broach such a subject—

perhaps it's her way of discussing the elephant in the room? It's an elephant that's been there ever since she chose Dolion as her lover. Prior to that, it was a toss-up as to whom that role would be assigned—either Jack or myself. Perhaps even both of us. "Dolion told you as much, didn't he?"

She nods against my shoulder. "Right before he took my virginity. That makes me only his."

I pull up to my elbow and look down at her where she lies below me. She turns so she's facing me and her expression is a curious one. "You belong only to yourself, no one else. You can choose whomever you like, whenever you like."

Confusion crosses her face, and she breathes out a troubled sigh. "I have… wanted both Jack and you," she admits. "But then Dolion and I…" she loses her train of thought and shakes her head. "I know this sounds odd, but I don't remember ever making the decision to be with just Dolion or, really, to be with him at all."

"I don't understand."

She nods as if to say she can understand how her comment is confusing. "It was just that… we were arguing and then before I knew it, he was kissing me and confessing feelings and then it was almost as if I had no will against

149

him. He was suddenly inside me and all the while, I didn't remember ever having wanted it." She clears her throat. "And from that moment on, it was as though he claimed me and I was his and that was the end of the subject."

"It certainly seemed that way."

She nods as she looks up at me. "It's strange, Claude, but I feel as if my head is clouded every time I'm near him—as if my thoughts are foggy and I can't think fully. But here and now, it's as though I'm back in control of myself."

"That is quite strange, indeed, and I don't know what to make of it." Then I breathe out a sigh. "The only reason I have for you is that Dolion is a force unto himself—and perhaps you simply lose yourself when you're near him because he's so all-encompassing. I know I often feel the same way, myself. It's as if whatever I need or want at the moment no longer matters and his will overcomes my own. But, the strange part is, I never notice it until the subject has passed."

"Right," she says and nods. "It's perplexing."

"It's just the island that is Dolion."

She nods. "I suppose my reason in saying all of this to you is an apology."

"An apology?"

"For choosing Dolion over you. Even

though I… I never remember making that decision, but I must have… obviously."

"What's done is done," I answer and give her a smile. "Though, for the record, I would not have minded sharing you with Jack," I add with a shrug. "Neither would Jack have minded either, for that matter."

"Truly?"

I nod. "Men and women in our native Wonderland generally have more than one sexual partner. We're rarely monogamous. From what I've observed, I imagine even your ghost would seem content with such an arrangement."

"But Dolion," she starts.

"Doesn't subscribe to the say beliefs, yes, I know," I interrupt.

She nods, but her eyes appear confused, "Dolion loves me."

"Maybe once he could have," I answer, shaking my head because I have no doubt that Dolion's ability to love is long past. "But I doubt Dolion loves anyone now."

"He says he does," she insists. "That's why he was so furious with me about nearly kissing Jack."

"Look," I reply, watching her face. "Let's get some sleep now. That should be your primary focus."

She nods. "I just… wanted you to

understand."

"I understand."

She lays her head back down on the pillow, but instead of closing her eyes to sleep, she stares at something in the distance. When she speaks, her voice is distant.

"You don't believe Dolion loves me."

I clear my throat, uncomfortable with this discussion. "What does it matter what I believe?"

"Because I trust you."

"I believe if Dolion really loved you, he would accept you just as you are. And he wouldn't dictate his terms as if you're no more than a soldier in his army."

"I thought I *was* a soldier in his army?" she replies with a little laugh, tinged with some despair.

"Wonderland teaches all its children that, despite the similarities, love and war are very different pursuits. You can be loyal to your own side in the fight without being chained to your commander emotionally."

Tears fall down her face again. It's hard to say why. Is she uncertain of my answer? Or is she crying because she feels understood? Clearly, she's wrestling with considerable turmoil beneath her lovely face. I wipe the teardrops away with my fingers, looking down at her thoughtfully. She's so simple and yet so complex at the same time. And I've no doubt that I'll protect her to the ends of the earth if necessary.

She leans forward to kiss me, but I pull away.

"Please," she whispers.

Yes, I'm concerned about Dolion finding us, but as soon as I look into the depths of her eyes, I realize I no longer care if Dolion does witness us—not when the love between Bowie and me can't be denied. Yes, I will stand up to Dolion if she won't.

I lower my head and claim her lips with my own. She's timid, at first. But soon she seems to draw energy from my response, demanding more from me. Her mouth probes mine and her hands explore the hard planes of my chest.

"Will you make love to me?" she whispers breathlessly, her eyes pinning my soul. Who am I to refuse such a request?

Chapter Fourteen
Bowie

Claude takes his time undressing me, kissing every inch of my heated skin as he exposes it.

I lie still beneath him, enjoying his touch as he slowly discovers my body. He palpates my breasts, cupping each one in his hands before kissing them individually, and making me pant in short, shallow breaths.

The quick thought that maybe I should be concerned if Dolion finds us crosses my mind, but I decide I don't care if he does. In fact, there's something angry deep inside me when I start to think of Dolion— something that wonders if he has some sort of control over me? Is it simply what Claude says—that Dolion is strong-willed? Does that, then, make me weak? Maybe this is my own form of rebellion?

Don't think of Dolion, I tell myself. *Focus on the here and now—focus on Claude.*

Drawing in a deep breath, I watch how Claude suckles one of my nipples and then the other, turning them into hard, pebbly buds. My reaction to his teasing throbs directly in my center, and my longing for him aches between my legs. When he caresses my thighs, my swollen clit pulsates, begging for his attention. But he takes his time to examine me inch by inch before locking me in another heated kiss. I can feel his hard cock pressing against my thigh while his body lies on top of mine.

I moan as he slips my panties free, dropping them onto the floor next to my other articles of clothing. "Why am I the only one undressed?" I ask.

"Impatient, are we?" he chuckles.

"Mmm, yes."

"Good things come to those who wait."

"Then I will wait forever," I reply with a slow smile.

My naked body is begging him to have his way with me. I just… I need to know what love can be with another man—with someone other than Dolion. I need to understand what I'm denying myself by pledging myself only to Dolion, someone whom I can't say I fully trust. But those are feelings I can't focus on at the moment.

Now there's only Claude.

I watch him kneel between my legs, pushing my knees apart to lie between them. His eyes don't leave mine as he trails his fingers inside my wet folds and the expression in his eyes is mischievous.

He plants his lips at my opening, dipping his tongue slightly inside me to taste me. A great, jolting shock bolts through my body. He continues to tease me and I reach down to comb my fingers through his messy hair, while I watch him softly lap my folds with his masterful tongue.

I arch back and nestle my head against the pillow, lifting my hips forward and higher as he becomes more aggressive in his exploration. He slips his fingers alongside his mouth and I moan loudly as he uses both fingers to massage my inner walls.

I'm so close to climaxing, but I hold back, savoring the crescendo of pleasure until I can't resist him any longer. My fingernails clasp the sheets on either side of me as I surrender to him. My body convulses with the force of my orgasm and I pulsate in glorious waves that start in my center, and ripple out, leaving my legs weak and unsteady.

He smiles at me from between my legs before pulling himself higher to kiss me.

He's rock-hard now, and I can feel the head of his sizable cock just at my entrance, as if begging to push into me.

"Yes, Claude," I whisper.

In response, he pushes deep inside me while he continues to kiss me in a way that betrays his depth of feelings for me. He loves me and I can feel as much in the union of our bodies. What's more—I love him.

He begins a slow rhythm but quickly grows more urgent. I gasp as he fills me completely, pushing as hard as he can. His strokes return to being slow and deliberate and his lips fall against my neck. He takes a brief pause because he can feel the fact that my body is suddenly tense. He looks down at me with concern in his lovely eyes.

"What's wrong?" he asks at my hesitance.

"Nothing," I reply breathlessly, although I must admit to feeling guilty because I know this will upset Dolion. He'll feel betrayed by my infidelity. Yet, I can't stop myself. And I also can't lie to myself—I feel something deep for Claude, just as I do for Sinbad and for Jack. I love each of them in their own way, in my own way.

I forcefully push my guilty thoughts away, losing myself in how good Claude feels inside me. He hastens his pace, pumping in and out of me with long, fluid strokes, building up the anticipation as his own need for release pulsates inside me. He speeds up, thrusting harder as he holds tightly onto my breasts. His thrusts betray his own desire for me—all this time he's wanted me just as much as I've wanted him.

"Oh, gods," he tells me at last and by the evident strain on his face, I can see he is close to claiming his own release.

"Yes," I coax him, and my previous guilt over Dolion is instantly swept aside in the maelstrom of pure ecstasy that glosses over Claude's face.

He finishes with a few deep, slow strokes, sinking fully inside me when he ejaculates. All the while, he manages to push me over the edge one more time, making my body shudder with another orgasm.

Afterward, we lie together, still connected, just listening to each other's heartbeats.

"We should dress," Claude says as he sits up. "Jack and Dolion," he starts to explain as I nod.

At the mention of Dolion's name, guilt floods me, but it's not something I can focus on long. I just, somehow, can't imagine that what Claude and I just shared is wrong. Not when it feels so right. Not when there is so much caring and kindness between us. Not when there's so much love between us.

"How did you get all these scars?" I ask Claude as I watch him pull on his breeches. I outline a long scar that starts on his abdomen and reaches all the way around his right side.

"I, um… hmm," he mumbles with a puzzled expression. "You know, I can't remember now."

"How can you forget how you received a scar that large?" I laugh, shaking my head because I can't understand how that can be.

"That's a good question, and I wish I had a good answer. As you can see, I've got a lot of scars."

"I can see that," I say, playfully spanning my fingers across his broad back. He's right—his body is literally covered with scars. "But this one is massive. It must have taken a long time to heal."

"I'm sure it probably did, but I can't remember any of the details now. In the haze of battle, things just bleed together after a while."

I frown at him because his words don't make sense with the display on his skin before me. "But you aren't a warrior. You're a man of the cloth."

158

"I *was* a man of the cloth—once—a long time ago. Not so much anymore. And I've been a pawn in this fight for quite a while now."

"Yet you can't remember how you survived such an extensive scar?" It seems odd to be sure. And I'm not certain if he isn't lying to me. Yet when I look into his eyes, I only see truth there. He honestly doesn't remember.

He shakes his head. "No, I really can't."

"Don't you think that's strange?"

"I suppose so, but when experiences are horrible, we tend to block them out."

"Yes, I understand that," I reply. In fact, that's what I'm doing right now. I wish I could forget the horror of the battle I just engaged in by losing myself in Claude's body and the smile he wears just for me.

Chapter Fifteen
Dolion

Much though I don't want to admit it, I must face the fact that Jack and I are stuck exactly where we are for the time being.

In doing our reconnaissance, we ended up putting ourselves into a precarious situation of being surrounded by enemies on all sides. Luckily, they don't realize we're here—stuck in the midst of the forest, but we could easily alert them to our location if we attempted to leave. Thus, we'll have to stay put for the time being—until the soldiers leave. I don't imagine that will take long as it seems, from what we could tell, that they were simply regrouping and would soon be marching North.

Bowie deserves praise for taking out so many of the enemy at once. But according to Jack, that's just the start of what he believes she's capable of doing. He believes she has more power than any of us are aware of. With a little more practice and free rein, she can do so much more.

Jack and Claude represent the highest standard of all the Guild members in my acquaintance, and the most capable of training a Chosen One to achieve their full potential. So far, they've done an outstanding job.

Even so, I can't help but think what's going on between Claude and Bowie now, while they await us in that damned cabin. I've seen the way Claude looks at her—the desire in his eyes. And I also know how fond Bowie is of him. While I've done my best to keep her by my side at all times, there's nothing I can do now. If they choose to enjoy one another, I can't stop them. And that realization burns me like all the fires of hell.

It's unfortunate Bowie doesn't realize it, but neither Claude nor Jack nor the errant soul she carries around like a circus balloon are worthy of her. None of them deserve her. She belongs to me and no one else! I would cut down every last one of them before I allowed them to touch her.

And yet, there's nothing you can do to stop Claude from taking her now.

If he's so much as touched her, I'll kill him, I think to myself. *Not only would it be a sign of disrespect to me, but she's mine!*

Closing my eyes, I think of Bowie's perfect skin, those large blue eyes, pert nose and rosebud mouth. I think of her tiny frame, so delicate and fragile, yet in full possession of unparalleled power.

Luckily, Jack is off in the distance, tending to a call of nature, so I'm alone. Thus, I slip my hand inside my pants to adjust myself and the effects of my yearning for her. I try hard to ignore thoughts of her for the time being, but it's no use. I'm illogically consumed by my lust for her. I release my aching cock from its confinement and begin stroking myself as I imagine her soft skin and ample curves and the feel of her wet and slick channel as I push within her.

I remember how she tastes. How she feels, her body so tiny against mine. I wish I were tangling my tongue lazily with hers until everything around us drifts away. I can just imagine gently lowering her onto the grass, away from the others, hidden by the tall reeds.

I would slip the straps of her dress off her shoulders, kissing her breasts, and taking my time with her. Her scent and the natural wild aromas of nature around us would blend into an unexpected aphrodisiac that would make us succumb to our passions. I can feel my lips alternating from one nipple to the other, planting warm kisses and suckling her hardened buds. My hand would drift down, slipping underneath her undergarments, which would already be soaked; I'd know she was ready for me.

"I missed you," I would tell her.

"I missed you too," she would reply. "I saved myself for only you, Dolion. I am yours. Forever."

"Yes, you are mine and mine alone."

She would nod. "No other man can compare to you. Forever."

Forever.

It's a word that thrills me—that causes me to climax—right there, whilst standing in the middle of the forest with the enemy surrounding me. What a vile thing to do! Masturbating like a horny teenager who caught a wee glimpse of knickers under a young noblewoman's skirt!

I'm disgusted with myself. How dare I sully Bowie with a grotesque display of self-flagellation! But I need her so much now, like oxygen. She means everything to me, and she's become my greatest possession. Nothing will ever stop me from keeping my hold on her.

Jack is moving around nearby, no doubt, hunkering down for the night in a dark alcove where he won't be discovered. I wash myself off in the narrow stream nearby, cleaning off all the evidence for which I despise myself, before returning to our makeshift camp.

The horses are secured a short distance away. Hopefully, they'll remain undiscovered during the night so we can begin our return to Claude and Bowie at first light.

And as to Claude and Bowie, if she accepted the arms of another despite my love for her, then may the gods help her. I can't imagine what I'll do if she forsakes me. I can't lose her now. I won't allow that to happen.

If necessary, I'll hide her away in a place of isolation until she learns to love me as much as I love her. Given enough time and solitude, I know she will.

Sinbad

As I was advised—or rather, commanded, depending on one's point of view—I've been keeping my distance from Bowie since the start of the battle. The shockwave I so graphically experienced in the ether I inhabit revealed the wisdom of her decision. It was painful for me to watch Claude carrying her away from the dangerous soldiers she inflicted such harm upon. But that was less than a bee sting compared to the pain of watching the intimacy I just witnessed between them.

Perhaps that seems odd, given the fact that it's quite clear she's been having a relationship with Dolion, but I've grown to accept that over the two weeks of the relationship's development. And I can't say that I believe wholeheartedly that Bowie was in her right mind when she made the decision to be with Dolion. There's just something different about her when she's around him—when I try to speak with her, it's as though she can't hear me. I know she knows I'm still there, as she'll smile at me and make small talk, but that seems to be the extent of our communication. And it's been this way for at least the last two weeks.

At first, I believed it was her way of dealing with the upset she knew I would have with the realization that she'd given herself to another man, but now I don't believe that was the reason. Instead, it's almost as though Dolion has some strange power over her—that she's completely obsessed with him. But only when he's near her. When she's alone (which is rare because Dolion watches her like a hawk), she appears to be the same Bowie we've all grown to know and love.

But back to Claude and Bowie and the lovemaking between them—I drifted in behind them when they entered the shelter and stayed hidden in the shadows. And witnessing her with another man stirred up another unpleasant revelation I'd been doing my best to avoid. What I want from Bowie, what I wish with all my heart, can never be. I can never have anything with her because of the fact that I am dead and she is not.

That inescapable fact haunts me constantly, and it goes far beyond my petty, little wishes, though "little" is an understatement when I try to describe how those feelings affect me. I love

Bowie and I would do anything for her and though I know she loves me too, our love is limited. Ultimately, it's impossible.

And, truly, if Bowie is to end up with another man, which she inevitably will, Claude is a good one—he would protect her and cherish her just as she deserves. I can't say the same for Dolion.

Regardless, Bowie has some decisions in her future. I clearly remember how it feels to go into battle for the first time—the uncertainty, and regret, and longing for an innocence that will never return. There was little I could do to prepare her for it and now that the damage is done, I fear she might not ever be the same. Of course, Claude fed her kind words and hopeful statements. But who knows whether that will help her psyche? It's one thing to prepare for an event and another thing entirely to experience that event. And when said event is taking the life of another? It's something you never forget.

For now, I must stay close to her. Close, but out of the way. I'm here if she needs me— as a confidant and friend. I would like to think I'll always be the one she seeks to confide in, but I know better. I know better because that most unpleasant revelation persists, despite how hard I've been batting it aside—eventually, I must cross the barrier into my afterlife and then I will lose Bowie forever. And that's a moment

I can't even contemplate.

Even now, as I watch Bowie lying in Claude's arms, I wonder what they might mean to each other. I'm not so callous as to try to listen to their words, so it's more than a shock when I hear Bowie call out, "Sinbad?"

I make no attempt to hide and instantly slip from the shadows toward the two of them. Claude, understanding man that he is, nods to Bowie and to me (well, at least he nods to the area he believes me to be in) and then excuses himself from the cabin, saying he wishes to see if there's any sign of Jack or Dolion.

"I'm so happy to see you!" she says, her grin bright and beaming. There are unshed tears in her eyes and all at once, I realize how much I mean to her, even though I'm in this blasted incorporeal state.

"I'm happy to see you too," I answer in a small voice. I wish more than anything that I could take her in my arms and hold her—feel her. But, alas, some things are impossible.

"Are you all right?" she asks me.

"As well as can be expected," I tell her truthfully. "And you?"

Her face clouds with uncertainty. "I'm not sure." Then she looks more closely at me and says, "I don't know what to think about how I feel."

"Then try your best not to think about it," I

answer. "And focus on the future and the experiences that lie ahead."

"The experiences that lie ahead are exact echoes of the one I just had," she answers as her shoulders sag. Then she looks up at me. "Either way, I promise you that as soon as we are finished here, I will escort you to your forever after."

She says the words as if she believes I want to be escorted to my forever after. That I actually want to leave her side.

"You may not be in a position to—"

"I just sent countless men into the ether without any direction or guidance. I won't let you wander there too!" Her voice catches and I realize she's barely holding back tears. "Please, Sinbad. Try to hang on a bit longer."

"I've been doing nothing less than that," I assure her.

Bowie worries her lower lip as she faces me and shakes her head, tears still threatening those beautiful eyes.

"I… I want to tether you to me again," Bowie says and I simply nod as she closes her eyes and reaches out to me and I feel our souls uniting once again.

###

Jack

The next morning, I notice Dolion is agitated by something; however, I can't be bothered with coddling him just now. Bowie is much better at that, anyway. Despite Dolion's protests, I insist that we scout the next camp before we return to the cabin—first, we must make sure where our enemies are located.

I can understand Dolion's burning need to check on Bowie, especially because it's no secret that Claude wants her—maybe even more than I want her. But Dolion needs to think of what's at stake at the current moment, should we be spotted. His thoughts shouldn't center around the potential cuckoldry he might have just received.

At the thought, I find myself chuckling. Truly, I hope Claude buried himself inside Bowie's tightness. I hope he rutted her repeatedly and filled her with his ejaculation. And if he did, I really hope he'll give me all the details. Claude is a private man, in general, but the two of us have become close in our travels and I believe he would let me in on his secret.

I do believe that were it up to Claude and me, the two of us would willingly share Bowie—such is our way in Wonderland. Unfortunately, though, Dolion doesn't see things quite the same way—he views people as possessions.

Though I've certainly pledged myself to Dolion and I've been his loyal companion and warrior all this time, I feel my fealty towards him dimming. Ever since I saw the way he treats Bowie—how he acts as if he owns her, I've lost respect for him.

As these thoughts penetrate my mind, I believe the vision before me—that of Bowie and Claude coming towards us—is nothing more than a creation from my mind, the outcome of not enough sleep and too much worry. Yet, the closer they come, the more I realize they are real. They've found us!

As soon as we spot them, I can see Dolion's eyes narrow on Claude. He says nothing in greeting to our Guildmember, but walks up to Bowie and nearly yanks her off her feet. That strange, haunted expression immediately overcomes her face, and she just smiles languidly up at him. He, meanwhile, hugs her as if she's a buoy, and he's floating upon a raging sea.

I can't seem to tear my attention away from her vacant gaze—it's the same thing that's been happening whenever she's in Dolion's company. If I didn't know better, I'd assume Dolion had somehow glamoured her, but I do know better—Dolion doesn't possess magic.

Regardless, Dolion immediately begins

sizing Claude up. After his previous reaction upon finding me with Bowie, I can only imagine his fury if he thinks the two of them were fooling around behind his back.

No doubt about it, Dolion's jealous streak is broad and deep. It's not a good trait in a warrior, much less a leader. It's the reason most men in our circles refuse to lay claim to just one woman and likewise. Sexual conquests must be relegated to a low priority if one intends to prevail in war. Well, whatever Dolion's thinking, he needs to stop. If we fail in our mission, whoever had sex with Bowie first, last, or most often won't matter.

Thankfully, no one brings the subject up. Instead, we devise a plan to attack the next camp and prepare to do so at sundown.

Chapter Sixteen
Claude

I can't make sense of my thoughts.

There's something blocking them, but I can't quite put my finger on what that something might be. Perhaps there's a witch trying to penetrate my mind? These forests are known for housing hags—female magic users who spin their charms for evil ends.

Regardless, I keep getting flashes of battles I don't remember, like bad dreams, but they seem far too real. I'm supposed to be fighting for the Guild, but the men I'm battling in these brief flashes are members of the Guild.

Is it a premonition of a civil war within our ranks? But, no, that can't be right. Why would we turn on one another at this crucial time? And why do these flashes or visions feel more like something that's already happened rather than something that has yet to occur? Most importantly, what in the nine hells is wrong with me?

I sit up and notice dawn overtaking the sky.

Even with the break of a new day, I vacillate between feeling terrified by what I remember of the dream and being relieved it's over. Another nightmare. They've been happening every night since the first battle after my tryst with Bowie. My now-familiar dream scenario sees me running from something big and powerful. I want to say it's Morningstar, but I don't know for sure.

Perhaps my nerves are getting the better of me. Bowie did her part to bring down the enemy in the last battle, but there are still more to come. That gives her more chances to rise or fall. But the image of a Guild civil war stubbornly clings to my brain. I sense there's something else in our midst, something I must protect not only Bowie from, but everyone else in the realm. I can't identify the powerful force yet, but I can certainly feel it. One thing I do know about this darkness—if it catches me, I'll be consumed, consigned to a dark, foggy void from which there's no escape.

I get up and dress, eager to return to the trail and let the fresh air clear my head. Usually, I find some clarity after the nightmares subside, and I've had a moment or two to prepare for the day. But on this morning, nothing seems normal. I can't tell where the nightmare stops and reality begins. The fog in my head seems like a cloudy mist in a deep valley.

173

I feel a pang in my guts as I see Bowie before we move out. I don't know why, but I have this horrible feeling she's in trouble. Yet, there's no trouble I can see. There's nothing I can save her from because whatever this threat is—it's not yet arrived. At least, that's how it feels.

"Good morning, Claude," she says brightly, her eyes shining in the sun as it rises.

"Good morning," I reply, quickly giving her a smile in return.

The smile we share is secretive, one of understanding that what passed between us must remain between us. I hope things won't remain as such for long because I want to eventually be able to revel in my love for this woman. Yet, we both know now is not a good time, not when we're headed back into battle.

As I saddle up, Jack helps Bowie with her saddle. I watch them, and a pain begins in the back of my skull—a throbbing ache. The pain has nothing to do with the two of them—but I have a feeling it has to do with the fogginess of mind to which I awoke. I make a mental note to consult a healer when we pass through the next town, whenever that might be.

I feel another rush of fog stealing over my mind, as if the first attempt wasn't good enough. This fog feels as if it's traveling through my brain and stealing my memories, leaving me confused and sluggish, in pain and ill. As I try to think back to my distant history—to my boyhood, no images come. No memories, no visions of my past. I try to picture my mother's face and it's much the same. It's as if a brain beetle was granted entrance into my head in order to feed upon the gray matter between my ears.

I try to content myself by watching Bowie from afar, appreciating her beauty and her power, attempting to forget whatever this darkness is that's come over me. There's no use in panicking—doing so will accomplish nothing. Yes, I need to visit a healer as soon as we enter the next village.

Bowie… why do I feel this sudden anxiety where she's concerned? Why do I feel as if I'm hiding something?

I rack my brain and find the memory hidden in a far-off corner.

We've had to keep our tryst silent

Tryst… tryst… what tryst?

You made love to Bowie, Claude, the answer arrives and I wonder at how unfamiliar it feels.

Yet, if ever Dolion was watchful where Bowie was concerned before, he's even more so. In fact, I think he believes something passed between the two of us because he's been suspicious and distrustful of me ever since we found each other again. And, I suppose, for good reason.

Good reason because you're in love with her.

Right. I'm in love with her.

I can't think on Dolion long—not when my head aches as it does. Instead, I'd much rather focus on Bowie and do so in the most concealed manor. She's a much better warrior than any of us ever expected her to become. I feel proud to observe her in her role as one of the Chosen.

What is her role as a Chosen One again?

Blast! I can't remember! And I also can't get this damned fog to clear.

After we've ridden for a while, Dolion calls out, "You all right, Claude?" His voice sounds so far away, like he's in a void, and I find him almost hard to comprehend. I can see his mouth moving, but the words coming from his lips might as well be gibberish. I can't understand a damned word! Gods, I'm slipping further and further away!

What in the nine hells is wrong with me?

"I think I… need to see… a healer," I manage to reply, but every word takes extraordinary effort.

Dolion slows down, pacing his horse with mine, and speaks in a low tone so the others won't hear. I can't understand what he's saying. His words make no sense, but he speaks them in a fevered, hushed tone. The fog swirls and bogs down my addled brain with increased ferocity. Unable to resist it any longer, I surrender.

###

The next thing I'm aware of is Dolion and I standing at the door of a cottage on the edge of the woods. I have no idea how we came to be here or where we are. It's simply as if I blinked and my surroundings changed.

"Claude, can you hear me?" Dolion is speaking to me again and this time I can understand his words. I nod and then glance around myself, trying to understand where I am. I notice our horses grazing nearby.

We're alone. "Where are Bowie and Jack?" I manage.

"I've brought you to the healer, Claude," Dolion answers.

"The healer," I answer, shaking my head because I can't understand what's happening to me. Why am I at the healer's? Is something wrong with me?

Whereas before there was nothing but clouds in my mind, now I can focus and comprehend perfectly well. "I can hear you much more clearly now," I say as I look around. I can't help but continuously focus on the fact that it's just the two of us. I'm suddenly worried for Bowie. "Where's Bowie?"

Dolion's eyes seem to darken after I mention her name. His jaw tightens and there's something in his eyes—something angry. "She went with Jack and her phantom to gather provisions for the next leg of our journey."

I have torn feelings about that news. Her distance from me means I can't protect her. And I fear she'll enter the next battle without me unless I clear my mind at once. But my thoughts make no sense anymore. The madness of Wonderland is the only thing comparable to this, except this is worse, no matter how unbelievable that sounds. My malady comes with a horrible sense of dread that refuses to subside, a panic of impending doom. Yet I can't remember why.

It's that awful fog—it's returned with a vengeance.

"Claude?" Dolion says. I suspect it's not the first time he's called my name after my initial response.

"Yes?" I say slowly, my voice sounding foreign as the fog begins to clear slightly and allows me to think.

"Ah, there you are! I thought I lost you again."

"No, not yet anyway."

"Can you tell me what might be causing this?" Dolion asks.

"I wish I knew."

"When did it start?"

"The night of the first battle." Suddenly, the fog starts distorting my memories. "Wait, no, I was fine that night. It started... It must have started the next day. After Bowie and I met up with you and Jack."

His eyes further narrow and it seems as if flames of anger flutter through them. His jaw is now even tighter. "Were you intimate with Bowie the night before this illness befell you?"

It's the first time he's come right out and asked me this and I'm shocked. Shocked and I don't know what to say.

"Um," I reply, hesitant to say more. Even in my befuddled state, I clearly remember what Bowie said about Dolion's claim on her. Stil,l if something happened that night, something that has to do with the horrible fog that now dominates my mind, it's important I say something.

"Claude, I need to know the truth," Dolion says, echoing my own thoughts. "Were you and Bowie intimate?"

I look up at him then. "Yes, I was," I answer finally, figuring there's no reason to continue walking on eggshells around him. He'll have to handle the fact that I love Bowie and she loves me.

"Is that so?" Dolion replies through gritted

teeth.

"Yes," I answer, but the word seems to come from someone else's mouth. The fog is circling again, threatening to overpower me.

"Then you have your answer," he says, still glaring at me.

"My answer?"

He chuckles then, but there's nothing funny about the sound. "What you're experiencing— it's a side effect of having sex with Bowie," he says with authority. "She did this to you."

"I don't... I don't understand."

"Her power... it's polluted you."

I don't understand how that's possible and, furthermore, how her power hasn't polluted him when he's had sex with her more times than anyone can count. Yet I also can't seem to find the words to argue with him. The fog is in full swing now.

"I'm leaving you here with the healer," Dolion says. "You must let him treat you."

"All right," someone, probably me, responds.

"Very good," Dolion replies through the fogginess.

I hear a knocking sound, but whether it comes from inside or outside my head is unclear. It echoes and I also hear a voice coming from nearby. The speaker talks in a hushed tone and addresses Dolion, who

responds in an equally small voice. My brain
has difficulty filtering through the miasma and I
soon abandon the extreme effort it takes to
listen.

"Claude," Dolion says. "The healer will
have you back on your feet in no time. Do you
understand?"

"I don't want to stay here," I manage to
reply. "I need to protect Bowie."

"No one needs to protect Bowie but me,"
Dolion responds, and his eyes are like ice. He
clears his throat and continues. "You are ill and
you need to be seen to. That's what's best for
you now, Claude. You understand, don't you?"

I want to say no, but I can't. "Yes," I
respond, or maybe I just think I say yes.

"Claude, do you understand what I'm
saying to you?" Dolion says louder.

I try my best to concentrate on his face
because it appears as a blur. Instead of one face,
though, I see two. They roll in and out of one
another, combining and separating, like an
ocean wave after it crashes onto the shore and
gets sucked back out to sea.

Chapter Seventeen
Bowie

"Where is Claude?" I ask when Dolion returns without him.

"He is feeling unwell," Dolion replies. "I took him to a healer to recover."

"Unwell? How so?" I ask, genuinely concerned for his well-being.

"The healer hasn't made any diagnosis. Claude was hallucinating, and he had some trouble speaking. Might be owing to some bad provisions he consumed."

"I've eaten the same food he has," I point out, "and I'm not ill at all. None of us are."

Dolion's eyes spark with a dangerous anger inside them. But he calmly replies, "Regardless, we can't afford to wait any longer. Those camps must be destroyed at once. He can join us again after his head clears."

"We need to wait for him," I argue, sensing something very wrong. "We *must* wait for him. Surely a day's rest and a tincture or potion of some sort will cure him quickly enough?"

"Bowie," Dolion replies with a vitriol I've never heard before in his voice. "I know about what passed between you and Claude in the cabin."

I'm surprised, but I let the shock pass. I'm not going to apologize for the love between Claude and me. "What of it?"

"It's your fault that Claude's ill," Dolion spits the words back at me.

I feel my heart drop down to my toes. "My fault?"

"You've made him ill because of your excessive power."

I shake my head because I can't understand how that can be. "I haven't made you ill and we've repeatedly bedded one another."

"My constitution is stronger than Claude's," Dolion answers, but the tone of his voice betrays his disbelief in his own words. I have nothing to do with Claude's malady—the truth is in Dolion's eyes. He might blame me, but even he doesn't believe his words.

Either way, I'm struck speechless. Thankfully, Jack isn't so easily silenced.

"How odd, Dolion. Only a moment ago, you claimed Claude's illness was due to something he ate."

"I was trying to be kind, as Claude himself would certainly be," Dolion retorts, glaring at Jack in a way I find unnerving. "But kindness will not end this battle. Our mission remains incomplete, so we must get moving again, with or without Claude."

"Very well," Jack replies, sounding slightly subdued. When I glance at him, I find him looking off into the distance. Perhaps he's embarrassed for being called out by Dolion.

"Let's be on our way now, Bowie," Sinbad whispers to me. His distrustful voice validates my own suspicions—there is something wrong here—something more. Dolion isn't giving us the full picture.

After we make camp for the night, I slip into Dolion's tent because I want to further discuss Claude and this strange malady that Dolion blames on me.

"Leave me be, Bowie," he growls when I approach him.

"You and I need to talk," I manage and even as I say the words, a strange feeling begins to pass over my mind, as if dissolving the anger and the emotions that were just wild within me a moment or so earlier. Instead, I look at Dolion and see him as the warrior and leader he truly is, and I'm suddenly ashamed that I could think to bother him with my silly quibbles.

"There's nothing to talk about!" he says.

"That's… that's not true," I respond as I search for the reason I came in here in the first place. Ah, yes… Claude. But what about Claude? Where is Claude? And why is Dolion so angry? Why did he make the choice to leave Claude when we should have waited for him to heal?

Dolion turns to face me then and there's rage in his eyes. "I told you I love you, and don't want to share you with anyone else."

"I love you too, Dolion," I answer automatically.

He chuckles, an ugly sound. "And yet you fucked Claude!"

Did I? Is that true? I can't imagine I would have done such a horrid thing when the man I love is standing right in front of me. "I don't…" I start, but I can't finish the words. It feels so difficult to talk, to even think.

"Do you love him?" he demands.

"I don't… know," I answer, shaking my head.

Dolion narrows his eyes at me. "Speak freely."

Then it's as if I've been doused by a bucket full of ice-cold water. I can suddenly think again, quite clearly.

"Do you love him?" Dolion repeats.

"Yes," I answer and then immediately feel the need to make him understand. "Love doesn't

185

diminish when you give it to another."

"You can't love more than one man at once," he argues, still glaring at me.

"You once loved another woman—the woman from the visions I had."

"So what?"

"So, you love her still and yet, you also claim to love me. How is my love for Claude any different from your love for her?"

"Unlike you, that woman's spirit is where it's supposed to be—in the beyond."

"I'm not trying to hurt you, Dolion," I say, hoping my gentler tone will make him understand me better.

"And yet you've succeeded," he answers and breathes in deeply. "I need to know if Claude is the extent of your... indiscretions."

"He is the only man I have allowed inside me, with the exception of you, yes."

"And Jack?" Dolion continues. "What are your feelings towards him?"

"I care for Jack."

"Do you want him inside you?" Before I can answer, he adds. "The truth."

"Yes," I answer and realize the word just sort of dropped off my lips as if it had a mind of its own. "And I love Sinbad."

"The spirit?" he responds, shaking his head.

I nod. "I loved Sinbad before I loved any of you."

"Sinbad is a spirit."

"So what? That doesn't mean I can't love him."

"And Jack?" Dolion asks.

I swallow hard. "I have feelings for Jack too, yes."

He looks at me and his eyes narrow again and all of a sudden, I'm overcome with feelings of shame. I can't believe what I've done to this man—that my infidelity has hurt him as much as it has.

"I'm sorry," I say as tears build in my eyes.

"Take your clothes off and bend over my bed," he answers with iron resolve. His eyes are piercing. "I'm going to show you just how angry I am."

I flinch at his command, temporarily caught off-guard by his fury. It's like a shockwave engulfing me, but I do as he says. And when he enters me, it's in one hard and long thrust. Our lovemaking that night is full of anger, pain and hatred, and I can't wait until it's over.

We leave early the next morning and Dolion rides ahead of us. He ignores me and I don't know what to do about him. The love I thought I felt for him is fast eroding, and I'm starting to wonder if I ever really loved him in the first place. Strangely, the cloudiness in my mind is changing—it's not as foggy as it was before, and the absolute love I felt for Dolion isn't really there anymore. It feels like a shadow of its former self.

Although he never admits it directly, I know Sinbad is afraid for me. So is Jack. And all of us worry for Claude.

"I don't trust him, Bowie," Sinbad says as he floats beside me.

"Dolion?" I ask.

He nods. "I believe there's more to Claude's mysterious illness than Dolion lets on."

"You do?"

Sinbad nods. "Seemingly the day after you and Claude are intimate, Claude develops a sickness that disallows him from traveling with the rest of us? How convenient."

"Then you think Dolion had something to do with it?"

"I don't know, but I wouldn't be surprised." He pauses a moment and then shrugs. "I know you tend to give all people the benefit of the doubt," he adds, in a gentler tone. "But I've known far too many men like Dolion. The orders he gives to those he commands must be followed to the letter or there can be dire consequences."

"I'm not one of his soldiers, Sinbad."

"Aren't you?"

"All right, I am on the battlefield, yes, but this is different."

"Your choices translate to his enemies, Bowie," Sinbad replies, his face growing graver. "He will kill your choices as swiftly as he will slay Morningstar's underlings. If that happens, you won't be safe with him."

"Dolion wouldn't hurt me."

"Perhaps not, but would he lock you away and give you no other choice but to be with him and him alone? Yes! I'd bet my life on it." Remembering his current state, Sinbad adds, "If my life could be wagered, of course."

"I don't… I don't know what to say."

Sinbad nods. "There's nothing to say."

"So what do we do?"

"Just continue to watch him. If he's guilty of anything, it will come out sooner than later."

Chapter Eighteen
Bowie

I change into the soft pajamas I find on the bed.

I'm not sure who they belonged to or whether Dolion provided them for me, but I also don't care. I'm just pleased to have them—and the bath I just delighted in.

After traveling day and night, Dolion allows us to stay the night in an inn above an old tavern in the smallest of villages we've seen yet. This town consists of the tavern, and a few residences dotted here and there among the countryside.

I have no idea where we are exactly, but I don't let that fact discourage me. Doing my best to shake off my doubts, I sit in front of the dressing table mirror and brush my wet hair. It's impossibly tangled after keeping it tied up in a bundle all these days on the road. I'm grateful I can wash it properly now. It's a surprise to me how something as simple as washing and brushing my hair can manage to make me feel so much better. Maybe too much. Something is imminently looming and I fear this temporary peace is about to be rudely interrupted.

But how or why or by what? I'm unsure. It's just this murky feeling that looms over me, like a proverbial dark cloud. Truly, my mind is a jumble of thoughts, all of which ram into each other. It's enough to give me a headache. But I can't even concentrate on my headache, not after the fact that I don't know how Claude is fairing—whether he's beaten his illness or it has beaten him.

While warming myself by the fire in my room, Dolion opens the door and approaches me. Jack is busily drowning his own thoughts in a tankard of ale downstairs or, at least, he was before I took my bath.

"Have you any word of Claude?" I start, but Dolion shakes his head. "I don't like it that we left him, Dolion," I continue. "It wasn't the right thing to do. We're a team and we should have remained a team. Leaving one of our own behind…"

But I'm unable to finish the thought as Dolion holds his hand up towards me.

"Calm yourself, Bowie," he says, and I'm overcome with the sudden feeling that everything is going to be okay. Everything will work out. There's nothing to worry about.

Everything's not alright! A voice within me

insists. *What about Claude?*

"Where is Claude?" I hear myself ask, but my voice sounds far away and rippling, almost like it's underwater. How strange.

"There's no sign of Claude," Dolion replies with a thick voice. "Nor will there ever be again."

I feel my stomach churn though my feelings of happiness still course within me, as if trying to convince me everything is okay and will remain that way. But underneath those feelings is something different entirely.

Claude…

"Is he dead?"

"No," Dolion says, shaking his head. "But he won't rejoin us, either. I made certain of that."

I can feel something bubbling up within me—something that threatens the otherwise happy mood within me. It's something angry and distrustful—not feelings I want to feel, so I try to beat the feeling back, but it's insistent. "Why?"

"Because *you* hurt him."

I've hurt Claude? How would I have done such a thing and why? "I don't remember doing anything to hurt him."

"You have and in hurting him, you've hurt me," Dolion insists. "Actually, you've hurt everyone on this mission. Your powers affect all of us."

I shake my head from side to side, not understanding how this can be. I've never wanted to hurt anyone, least of all Claude. He's only ever been kind to me.

"Deny it if you want," Dolion snaps. "But Claude's mind is irreversibly compromised, thanks to you. Now Jack is beginning to show the telltale signs of madness as well. Surely you've noticed."

All I noticed was an ever-increasing fatigue that seemed to be overcoming all of us. I thought that was the reason Claude wasn't well, but am I wrong? Is there a chance I *am* at fault for Claude's condition? I don't want to believe Dolion, but I can't help but wonder if maybe he's correct?

How could my nascent powers become so detrimental to the men I love?

I'm spared the chance to fully consider the subject when Sinbad suddenly appears to float through the door, in a panicked state. He doesn't appear to see Dolion, who stands off to the side and behind him.

"Bowie, we have to get out of here," he says. "Dolion isn't who—"

His body suddenly appears to fly backwards into the wall, though he simply goes through it, since he's a spirit.

"Sinbad!" I scream.

A moment later, Sinbad flashes through the wall again, reaching out for me with outstretched arms as a scream echoes through his mouth, reverberating against the wood planked walls. With horror, I realize he's being pulled back by a shepherd's crook!

Merciful Triple Goddess, he's being reaped! But by whom?

I take a moment to search for the tether that ties us together but I can't feel it. It's as if someone has severed it. I leap to my feet and run down the hall after him. Knowing Dolion won't do anything to help Sinbad, I shriek for Jack, who appears from the tavern momentarily.

"Bowie, what is it?"

"Sinbad's in trouble!" I reply anxiously.

I turn around then and spot Sinbad right behind me. And right behind him is the unmistakable silhouette of a shepherd. As I watch, in absolute horror, I see Sinbad being yanked down the stairs—well, as much as it's possible to yank a ghost down the stairs—that's the way it appears, anyway.

The shepherd stands at the base of the stairs and I can't see his or her face because a hood hides it. Strangely, the shepherd is as incorporeal as is Sinbad. It's as though they're both spirits, but that's impossible because a spirit can't reap another spirit.

Jack is quick to reach Sinbad. In fact, Jack

stands so close, he might be able to grab the crook and knock it away. He surges forward, reaching to grip the shepherd's hook, but it slips right through his fingers and the shepherd swiftly disappears, Sinbad with him.

"Outside!" I yell when I think I catch sight of the shepherd's crook bobbing along the treeline.

As we reach the edge of the gardens, the crook suddenly vanishes beyond the hedges. Then, before I can let out the breath I've been holding, several military men dressed in Morningstar's insignia rush forward, seizing Jack. He valiantly tries to fight them off, but he's outnumbered. As he fights to raise his hands and call on his magic, someone hits him so hard in the side of the face, he loses consciousness. Before I can come to his aid, another group of men ambush me, pulling me in the opposite direction of Jack. I can identify one member in the group that has Jack: the infamous Hassan. They begin dragging Jack away.

Act, Bowie! I yell at myself. *Call up your power!*

I have enough mental clarity to access my powers, but before I can, I'm plunged into sudden darkness when a heavy cloth is tossed over my head. Seconds later, my hands are bound behind my back. Vainly, I struggle to release myself when the men begin hauling me off.

I scream, hoping Dolion will hear me, but if he does, he never comes. After his last litany of cruel accusations, though, I wonder if he even cares about me any longer.

"Where are we takin' her?" one of the men asks.

"Morningstar wants her brought to the tavern," the other man replies.

My heart flip-flops in my chest.

Morningstar? He's here? I knew I'd eventually confront the bastard, but I never imagined it would be like this. Not alone.

I don't know what to think or do as I'm pushed forward, but I can only wonder if they've captured Dolion. I hope he's escaped so he can alert the Guild. And Jack? I can only hope he's still alive.

"What do you wish me to do with her, Excellency?" one of the men says as soon as we walk back into the tavern—I can tell as much by the sudden darkness, the change in temperature, and the dankness of the air.

"Pull the hood off and leave her with me," replies a familiar voice, making my heart drop down to my toes because I don't understand what's going on. "Then leave this place and let no one else inside. I want my privacy."

As someone pulls the hood from my head, I blink to find Dolion standing in front of me.

"I don't understand," I say, shaking my head.

He chuckles as he looks at me. "Really, Bowie, you can't be so dense."

And that's when it dawns on me. Dolion has been working for Morningstar all along—he's a spy! "Why, Dolion?" I gasp. "Why are you helping Morningstar?"

With a chill smile, he pulls out the soul stone and replies, "I'm not helping Morningstar."

I frown up at him, angry that he's going to try to lie to me when the truth is staring me right in the face. "At least show me the respect I'm due by not lying to my face," I say, spitting the words at him. "It's obvious you're in league with him."

Dolion glares at me. "I'm not helping Morningstar—I *am* Morningstar."

I'm in such shock, all I can do is drop my mouth open in disgust and surprise. "How did… how did no one ever recognize you?"

Then I wonder if anyone really knows what Morningstar looks like. I certainly didn't.

A small gem floats out of the soul stone and, holding it in his palm, Morningstar waves the stone in front of his face, changing his features instantly.

"It was simply a charm that changed my features," he explains.

The true form that is Morningstar is a massive figure that stands before me—towering well over seven feet. He has the shape of a man, but no one would ever believe him to be one—there's too much menace within his expression, his face. He appears as some sort of giant—bald head, beady little eyes of black and a wide nose and mouth. He's hideous.

"And the man you chose to look like?" I ask, shaking my head. "Dolion?"

Morningstar nods as if he expects this question. He turns to a wooden armoire that stands in the corner of the room, stretching to the ceiling. He walks up to it and, opening one of the doors, reveals a man I recognize to be Dolion. The man appears to be swimming in a sea of ice-blue water, suspended in a glass case. And he's asleep. Or dead.

"I had to keep his body alive in order to steal the essence of his likeness," Morningstar explains.

"Then he's alive?" I ask.

"Alive but without a soul," he answers on an exhale. "I saw to it that his soul was dispatched as soon as I stole his body."

"You're a monster," I growl, and tears fill my eyes.

"And what, pray tell, are you?" he snipes. "We're both monsters, but different sorts."

"I'm not the monster you are," I answer, trying to keep the tears at bay, but they roll down my cheeks, anyway. As realization dawns on me, memories begin filling my mind—questions about things I now begin to understand. "Then all this time... the feelings I felt towards you…"

"Were my magic using your emotions against you."

I swallow hard. "And Claude? Jack?"

"All I had to do was cast my spell on both Guild members so you'd believe we were who we said we were. They never knew I controlled them." He glowers audaciously.

"Then Claude was never a follower of Morningstar?"

"Never and he was never a man of the cloth either. I implanted that memory into his consciousness and made him forget all the others. Same with Jack."

"Why?"

"To confuse them. To make them fight themselves, doubt themselves."

"So you could remain in charge," I finish. He nods and I continue. "And Claude's sickness?"

"He got in my way," Morningstar answers. "He bedded you when he knew you were mine. That was enough for me to decide to oust him."

"Then he was never sick because of me? I wasn't the reason he had to see the healer, you were." Morningstar simply nods as I shake my head, trying to subdue the shock, but it's still there. "Is he… still alive?"

"I know not," he answers on a shrug. "And I care not."

I can only hope Claude is still alive and I promise myself that if I'm able to escape, the first thing I'll do is make sure Claude is okay. And that leads me to another subject…

"Am I'm not really a Chosen One?"

"You are," he answers on a nod. "That much is true. I just simply located you before my enemies did."

It's then that I remember picking up that tattered flag at the camp—picking it up because I expected to see Morningstar's insignia and, instead, I saw the insignia of the Guild. The realization is almost too much for me to handle and bile rises in the back of my throat. I look up at Morningstar with wide eyes and he throws his head back as a deep chuckle escapes his mouth.

"Yes, the camp you so efficiently destroyed? It was a Guild camp! The lives you took belonged to the people you claim to defend." His sneer widens into a snarl. "So, let's examine the evidence and I shall ask, who's the monster now?"

"Is that why you decided to show yourself now?"

He nods. "You were starting to figure it out—asking too many questions."

This news nauseates me. How many innocent people did I kill for Morningstar? Far too many. Worse still, I nearly fell in love with the enemy I swore to execute.

"No, I'm not the monster," I respond between the tears. "You are. You lied to me this entire time! You lied about loving me and you lied to me about my true mission. You fucked me for your own diabolical ends."

"Now, now, don't let your temper get the better of

you. Indeed, I have always loved you."

"How could you when you don't even know me?!"

"Don't I? At this point, I think I know you quite well."

I can only respond with a sullen glare. Blowing out a great breath from his broad nose, he says, "Indulge me for a moment and I will try to enlighten you."

"Enlighten me about what?"

"About my past."

I figure it's a good thing to keep him talking because it allows me more time to figure out just what in the hell I'm going to do. How am I going to free myself from this situation?

"I was once the ruler of the skies in a place far away from here. After a minor conflict of interest with another cosmic being, I was cast out and exiled. Not only could I never return to my home, but I was also forbidden from ever having a new one. No matter where I went, I was met with rejection. Along the way, my beloved was cruelly killed."

"Poor monster," I say in a mocking tone.

"Then I discovered Fantasia," he continues, ignoring me. "A land rich with magic and all of the resources I required to make a proper home for my people."

"I thought only you and your deceased beloved were cast out."

"Ah, did I omit that detail?" he asks on a chuckle. "Actually, there were a handful of loyalists who followed me into exile. All of them were lost, displaced, rejected and terribly angry gods from my home as well as the other places I tried to make a home. After we conquered Fantasia, I appointed Kronos in charge of the afterlife. He scoured the ether for my beloved's soul. I had to retrieve her. You know how it is, don't you?"

I refuse to dignify his jab at my relationship with Sinbad by giving him an answer. When I think of that brave, foolhardy spirit, my heart aches. Is he lost to me forever? Or will I find him again once I enter the ether at the end of my life?

"Anyway, you know the rest," he says. "The war broke out, so I never finished what I set out to do. Fighting against time, I did what I could to contain my loved one's spirit. I had to stop her from crossing over before I could join her. Kronos located her in the ether and I found a vessel to house her for safekeeping…" His eyes light up as a terrible feeling starts up from the pit of my being.

"No," I say, shaking my head.

He smiles and nods. "A small child by the name of Bowie Bachette received a portion of my blood and became a Chosen One. The *real* Bowie, however, I killed outright. Then I used her body and blood to fashion a marvelous container deserving of my beloved." His eyes soften slightly as he adds, "So you see, Asherah, you never belonged to anyone but me. Isn't it time you admitted and respected that?"

I can only stare at him, speechless. As he speaks, it's as though he unlocks a long-forgotten door inside my head and moments later, memories begin flashing across my mind. I see Morningstar and me together in other times, other places, and other worlds. Unfortunately, what he's saying is true. Yes, this could be magic, but I don't think it is. I can feel the truth in his words.

He smiles as he looks at me, and the expression is a triumphant one. And why not? He knows I'm no match for him now that he's in his rightful form. I have no hope at all of taking Morningstar down.

That's when I notice the amulet hanging around his neck, and I sense something familiar—I can feel something pulling me towards it. And that's when I realize there's something in the amulet—something I need. The swift rush of memories become a blur and I can't recognize anything within them at first. After another few seconds, I realize these memories detail many things I didn't know before, but need to know now.

As the seeds of a plan take root in my mind, fueled by the sudden knowledge of experience, I smile up at Morningstar, and move slowly in his direction. He watches me, uncertainty clinging to his gaze. He has no reason to fear me because I can't hurt him… or so he thinks. I gently reach out and stroke his cheek. Then I move closer to pull him into a heated kiss.

Chapter Nineteen
Morningstar

I'm not sure what my beloved is doing.

But when she pulls me forward, I quickly surrender to her kiss. Perhaps the realization of her true identity is all that's needed to bring her back to me. The kiss doesn't lie. Every bit of my love for her surges within it, and she gives that love back to me freely. I don't have words to express how grateful I am for that.

I know she's still angry with me. After all, I lied to her. But I did what I had to do to protect her and to save us. Everything I did and sacrificed was to find our new home… In the name of us being together again. She'll forgive me in time, when she realizes the reasons why I've done the things I've done. I moved mountains to get here, after all.

When she finally pulls away, she's smiling happily, as if truly seeing me for the first time. I suppose, in a way, she is. I can't change the amount of time it took for her to come around—after all, she believed she was someone else all her life. But I can change the way we are together from now until forever. This is the start of the rest of our lives together.

"You have to understand, my love," I explain. "I want us to be together forever. We will rule this place *together*."

"I don't know," Bowie, no, *Asherah* replies. "I love that you've gone to such lengths for me. But you must realize you left me among people I've grown to love. People I don't want harmed in any way."

I feel slightly annoyed by her compassion. And then I must remind myself this is Bowie speaking, not the woman I knew in my past. Of course, I knew there were bound to be changes to Asherah as she grew up in this strange land. I knew she would form associations and attachments, but I was more than sure I could lure her away from them—in returning her memories, I know she will become the woman she once was again… it's just a matter of time.

I must be patient.

"I can understand that," I say, careful to keep my true feelings hidden. "But you have to remember who you are, and where you came from, my love. You are so much better than any of these people. That's why your true destiny is to rule over them, not embrace them." I turn away for a moment before adding, "Perhaps I made a mistake in leaving you with them for so long. I should have kept you closer to me. That way, I could have molded you into the woman I need you to be."

"And what kind of woman is that?" she asks. Even though she feigns curiosity only, I can see the fire burning in her eyes. Yes, my Asherah lives in those eyes evermore. "You claim to love me, yet you didn't hesitate to use me as an instrument of death. Surely you knew I wouldn't be happy taking the lives of those I consider innocent?"

The sting of truth in her words is undeniable. A small error in judgment on my part, to be certain, and one for which we are both paying. But the other unfortunate part of the situation was that I needed her to take out that Guild camp—it was the largest of them all and that blow helped my forces immeasurably. But Bowie will have to understand that—in time, I believe she will. "Yes, you are right, of course," I admit. "But I never abandoned you, Asherah. I was sure you could put all the people you previously loved behind you when you remembered whom you truly are. And now that time has come at last! Now you must take your rightful place by my side."

"You make it sound so easy," she says wistfully. "But it's not like changing clothes."

"Now that you know the truth, why isn't it that easy?"

"What I've done is horrible," she says, meeting my eyes and I can see the pain in hers. It's a pain I don't understand. "We can lie about how necessary it was, but it doesn't change how ugly and inhumane it was. And hearing your ultimate goal is even more horrible still: enslaving humanity and purging all who don't bend to your will." She sighs. "It's… not right, Dol… er, Morningstar."

Distant echoes from another conversation we had long ago ring in my head. I ask, "How else can we make Fantasia our permanent home? Or don't you remember being deprived of shelter in those other worlds?"

"If I were once someone who felt the same as you," Asherah says, looking away and letting her sentence drift off. Then she locks eyes with me again and continues, "I'm not that person any longer, Morningstar. I refuse to kill anything indiscriminately, but most certainly not the people I've come to love."

No, no, no, no! This isn't the way it's supposed to go! She's supposed to agree with me, not continue playing the role I put her in. "Perhaps some things about you have changed," I say, my tone cold. "But once you're beyond the clutches of these peasants, I promise you'll feel more like yourself again. I know you'll come back to me, given enough time."

"Wasn't that the whole point of your grand reveal a few moments ago? Bringing me back to myself?"

"It was, and I would have done so sooner than later. Indeed, I tried to resist exposing my true identity to you until the time was right. But the moment you witnessed the Guild's flag lying upon the ground and began putting the pieces together, I couldn't hold back any longer." I pause for a moment as I witness the anger in her eyes. Anger directed towards me. This is not how this conversation was meant to go at all! "You consume me, Asherah. You are the only love of my very long, very lonely life." My sincerity and heart bleed from my words. Surely that's enough?

"I love you too, Morningstar," she replies sadly and I can see the truth in her words. Now that she knows who she is, she no doubt feels the love Asherah once had for me. "I just don't know if I can embody the former image of the woman you loved ever again."

I release a loud sigh. This isn't working. I need to convince her I'm right. I must give her a meaningful token of my undying affection. After a few moments of thought, I finally settle on my answer.

"Let's make a bargain, then," I propose. "If you'll abandon and forget the others you say you care so much about, and agree to join me in ruling Fantasia, I will spare Sweetland and the people who live there." I hold up my index finger. "However, in exchange for my protection of Sweetland, you shall agree to be mine and mine alone. Any person with whom you dalliance will die." I drop my finger. "Do you accept the terms?"

She purses her lips, her brows knitting deep in concentration as I await her answer. Finally, she smiles broadly before moving in closer for another kiss. Her kiss is passionate this time, and she follows it by pushing me down on the floor. I don't resist her advances, so completely smitten as I am with her.

The only problem I foresee is if Asherah continues to insist she's not the woman she was in times past. Now that she has another identity, I have to wonder if I can control or possess her the way in which I intend. I'm sure she's confused, although she already seems to accept the situation, and that's an important first step. I quickly get lost in her kiss and having her to myself.

As she lies against my chest, the energy between us begins to manifest. Our powers mingle together and create an electrical charge that surges and flows between our bodies—it feels as it always did and it's a reminder of the love that unites us—a love that has survived all this time.

"My love," I murmur softly, "I can't tell you how difficult it was to keep the truth from you. So often, I wanted to tell you my true identity as well as yours…" I pull away from her slightly so she can see how serious I am.

"Shhh," she says, brushing a finger over my lips. "There'll be plenty of time to discuss that later." Her lips press on mine again and she purrs, "Right now, I just want to savor how good it feels to be here with you. It's been so long…" Then her tongue dives into my mouth.

Her tongue is warm and inviting as she tangles it with mine, drinking me in, eagerly offering me the sweetness I crave. The electrical charge hovers all around us, converting our excitement into an enticing tingle. Waves of magic crackle through the air as our powers combine into one. It's a new beginning, and we're floating on the cusp of possibilities. Oh, how she makes me weak with desire. So very weak…

Wait, I begin realizing something doesn't feel right. My energy is waning far faster than it should. I'm exhausted, not just tired. The tingle I sense is more than just the manifestation of energy between us. While subtle at first, the pull of my life force grows stronger and more insistent.

By the time I realize what she's doing, draining the life force from me, it's too late. I resist, and try to pull away from her, but for such a small woman, she is extremely strong. She clings to me, holding her lips on mine as she continues to suck my essence from me. And I can see my essence leaving my body in a string of bright green light. It's as if she's inhaling it into herself, through our joined lips.

I can feel my face caving in, the skin and muscles collapsing inward. Soon they're nothing more than a thin layer of flesh covering the bone beneath. Thankfully, it's only on one side of my face, where her lips are now securely fastened in place. With a last-ditch effort, I shove her violently away.

The amulet around my neck is suddenly yanked away, her fingers groping blindly for any way to hold on to me. With what remaining energy I have left, I funnel my magic at her and she flies across the tavern, landing in a heap. My eyes are wide as saucers as I stare at her, clutching my severely damaged face. Were she anyone else, I would have slowly shredded her to death. As it is, I'm far too weak to do so now, nearly unable to move.

"How could you?" I ask, the drama of her betrayal evident in my voice.

"We all do what we must do," she replies, sounding cold. "Isn't that what you taught me when I was Bowie?" She's far more adept in her art of deception than I give her credit for.

"So," I say, struggling to pull myself up. "You prefer these worthless mortals over your soul mate?"

"There are many souls in the world," she spits icily, pulling open the amulet to reveal the soul stone within. "Far too many to have only one love."

"N-n-no," I sputter in vain. After all her years as a shepherdess, she must recognize the presence of her phantom, Sinbad, inside the stone?

She slaps the stone awake and then aims it at the empty form of what once was Dolion, where he floats in a glass case of magic. The reaction is immediate, the body of Dolion quickly shakes as Sinbad's soul fills it. A moment later, the glass case shatters and he falls to the floor. The magic that appeared to be water just simply dissipates into the ether. He's unstable on his feet when he attempts to stand.

"Bowie?" he asks as he looks up at her in confusion.

She reaches down and takes him by the hand, helping him up.

"Asherah, no," I whisper. I wish I could follow her, grab her and pull her back to me, but I'm beyond exhausted. She's taken much of my life energy and it will require many days of rest in order to restore myself. Damn her!

Bowie takes Sinbad by the hand and they both run out of the tavern and toward the back gardens.

211

Even though I scream for my men to apprehend them, I know it's already too late. They escape through the old encampment as I struggle to rise to my feet. I grip whatever I can in my walk through the tavern and out into the air. As I walk, the grass at my feet instantly yellows and dies. That is no surprise.

Everything I touch dies.

I used to consider it a virtue, but now it feels more like a curse. As Sinbad and Bowie disappear into the darkness, I am left with nothing but physical and emotional pain for my trouble. And that is the exact moment when I grow angry.

Very angry, indeed.

Everyone responsible for this outrage *will* pay.

Chapter Twenty
Jack

The fog pickling my brain slowly begins to lift.

When the temporary confusion passes, I find myself in a cell, guarded by several men I quickly recognize as Morningstar's goons. There's no getting around the unpleasant fact that I'll have to fight my way out of here.

Using the remnants of my magic, which is all my weakened state can muster at the moment, I slowly melt the door hinges and the lock. It's an old spell and, unfortunately, a tedious one. Roasting a whole stag would be faster. But it's quieter than blasting the doors open, and I'm not sure I have the power to accomplish that, anyway. I need more time to build up my physical and mental strength for the battle ahead.

I rack my brain, trying to remember when the fog of confusion enveloped it. I can trace the mind fog back to the first moment I came into contact with Dolion, and he recruited me on this excursion. Ever since then, my memories of a time before Dolion have become scarce and I've felt almost as if I'm existing on autopilot.

And I was not the only one who was feeling such a way. Claude was already experiencing the same symptoms. Like me, Claude couldn't remember any of his memories prior to his time with Dolion. It was certainly odd. I confided my concern to Dolion, who admitted he felt the same as I. When Claude disappeared, I feared the worst, despite all the assurances Dolion gave me to the contrary. Furthermore, I couldn't believe how cavalier Dolion was about our loyal companion's sudden and surprising illness. And to have left Claude behind—it was another of Dolion's moves that had dumbfounded me.

So, why didn't you fight it? I ask myself. Strangely, I have no answer. It almost feels as if I were unable to go against Dolion, but that makes little sense because I have always made my own way. And men have never intimidated me. Regardless, our future battles will prove all the more difficult without Claude, even though Bowie proved herself better prepared than we expected for the challenge.

Something is keeping me in this befuddled state. Dolion's dark hints that Bowie is the one responsible sounds too self-serving to be true. It's no secret that he's trying to keep Bowie to himself and believes all of us, even the spirit

214

before he was shepherded to the next world, to be threats. Now I wonder if anything Dolion said was true. If I stay strong enough, I can soon discover the truth for myself.

Maybe "soon" is the wrong word to use. The lock and hinges are gradually melting, but a few glances at the guards tell me they don't realize anything is amiss. That will give me the advantage of surprise, although I still have to fight my way out of here. And without any weapons! My native Wonderland put me in worse situations than this, but not much worse. I shall simply have to do my best.

I wait on the tiny cot near the cell door, sneaking peeks at the hinges and lock, which are finally beginning to shift and soften. When I see the door is ready to fall, I sustain it with my magic and it manages to stand on its own as I hear the footsteps of the guards approaching.

Now! I jump up from the cot and throw myself against the door, pushing it until it falls on top of the guard on the other side. Snatching the dagger from the trapped guard's belt, I quickly use it to pierce the heart of the other guard. He barely gurgles as I pull the blade out of his chest and he falls to the ground. Another approaches me on the right, so I whirl my dagger hand around and make a clean slice across his throat.

"You fucker," the trapped guard hisses at

215

me as he finally squeezes out from beneath the metal door. As soon as he's on his feet, he charges me, swinging a mace at my head. I duck the blow and raise my dagger at him. He gives me a backhanded blow that I dodge sideways at the last moment. That gives me the opening I need, and I jab the blade into his ribs and thrust upward.

He screams in pain and loses his grip on the mace. As it sails through the air, I cast a quick enchantment to seize control of it. Then I gesture downward with my fingers and the blunt weapon lands on top of his skull, cracking it open and giving him a nasty head wound.

I step over his body and run out to look for Bowie. I immediately spot her fleeing through a dilapidated garden and there's a man with her— Dolion? On the other side is the dark wood we came out of this evening.

The tavern we were previously staying in is no more than an illusion. What stands in its place is an encampment in the woods that I quickly recognize. When was I here, though? At the sound of angry men in hot pursuit, I can only follow Bowie through the dead garden.

When I catch up to her, I see she's accompanied by Dolion. But he seems very different now—less cocksure and more concerned for Bowie, who's crying inconsolably. There's no time to talk, never mind inquiring after what's bothering her. Instead, we all continue to run until we reach the encampment before we dare stop to take a breath.

As we move away from the camp, some long-buried memories suddenly return. I remember traveling beside Claude on Guild business. Were we ambushed? Yes! This is the very same encampment they brought us to, the one we're just now escaping from.

The slap of Bowie's hand on my wrist snaps me out of my reverie. "They're getting closer, Jack!"

"Yes, they are," I agree. My strength hasn't fully recovered, but I stretch one hand out to the decaying plants of the garden. Immediately, I create new life. Grass quickly grows along with weeds. Bushes blossom and even block off the pathways. Long-dead animals rise to life, their noise and confusion a good a match for the guards' sudden bewilderment.

Bowie gives me a smile before yanking on my arm to keep going. I feel somewhat weakened by the spell, but I don't stop. At least Dolion is with us...

More memories fill my head. Claude and I fought our ambushers, but we were quickly overcome. I feared we'd taken our last breath until we arrived at this camp. The man... Was he a man? Whoever commanded the guards put us under a spell. A spell…

Think, Jack! I yell at myself. *Think, dammit, and remember!*

And that's when the memories begin flooding my mind as if a dam has busted in the back of my head. Images and memories that had been long buried in a perpetual haze come back again, riding a wave of vengeance and anger.

I realize with a dawning horror that I've been living a lie for several months now. So has Claude. But who's to blame? Who did this to us? Those memories haven't yet returned.

As we get further away from the camp, I'm overcome with relief. This constant fog in my head had nothing to do with Bowie at all. I feel guilty for even considering she might have been the reason. Whoever did this to us has officially earned our undying wrath. But, at the moment, I can't concern myself with wrath or justice. Instead, I need to find the answers to two important questions: Why was a spell cast on us? And who was responsible?

Eventually, we're far enough away from the camp and into the forest to safely take a rest. But nothing can shield me from the torment of my thoughts. And, currently, those thoughts are centered around Claude.

Dolion took Claude to a healer, I think. *But was it really a healer?*

And what about Dolion? Something odd

keeps niggling at me.

That's when the revelation dawns on me. The camp that Bowie destroyed! I knew the camp we'd attacked looked familiar. It was the place where we'd camped before the ambush. It was a Guild camp! And the man who ambushed us may have called himself Dolion, but I know his real name: Morningstar!

With sudden realization freeing me from the cloud that has been inside my head, I focus on Dolion who walks beside Bowie and realizing the danger she's in, I charge him, knocking him off his feet and taking him to the ground in an instant.

"You did this to us!" I yell accusingly, raising my fist.

Bowie intervenes, catching my arm as she wedges herself between us. "Jack, stop! You don't understand!"

"I understand perfectly," I answer her. "This man was never our friend, and he isn't Dolion. This monster is Morningstar."

"Not any longer, I can assure you," Dolion says to me. His cadence and speech are very unlike the arrogant commander who deceived me.

"He's not Dolion," Bowie seconds. "He's Sinbad."

I pull away from him and frown, not understanding how this can be. "Sinbad?"

A broad smile stretches across his face. "Yes, my friend, I am Sinbad, though now in this borrowed disguise of flesh."

I look between him and Bowie. "Is Dolion... I mean, Morningstar inside there with you?"

"No," Bowie assures me. "Morningstar is still in the tavern."

I stare at her, still trying to make sense of it all. "How did you manage to put Sinbad's spirit inside Dolion's body?" I shake my head, as none of this makes any sense. "Last I saw you, Sinbad, you were being reaped by a shepherd."

"Rather than destroying me," Sinbad explains, "our foe foolishly placed me in the soul stone for safekeeping."

"And once I realized Sinbad was in the stone," Bowie adds, "I seized my chance to put him into Dolion's body."

I nervously glance behind us. "What became of Morningstar, then?"

"He's greatly weakened at the moment," Bowie says, following my gaze.

"But if his reputation is accurate," Sinbad adds, "he shall regain his strength rather quickly."

"That's why we need to get as far away from here as possible," she replies.

The sound of footsteps running toward us interrupts our conversation. The unmistakable voice of Hassan rises above the din, and his raspy orders make my blood run cold.

Sinbad puts a protective arm around Bowie. "Dearest, you're in no condition to battle with Hassan, and neither are we."

"We have to get away from them," Bowie whispers urgently, before all three of us are back on our feet again.

I can hear Hassan still in hot pursuit, but we've gained quite a bit of ground and I continue to weave my magic into the environment around us and in response, bushes and trees sprout up behind us, hindering Hassan's way. Eventually, we lose Hassan in the vast wilderness. I find some comfort in our alien environment, which is far too dense for Hassan to navigate easily.

As soon as we determine it's safe, we slow down to rest and catch our breath.

Chapter Twenty-One
Sinbad

At the moment Bowie pulled me from the soul stone and dropped me into Dolion's body, I felt it becoming my own. Granted, it took me a few moments to grow accustomed to having a body again, but because I hadn't been a spirit for *that* long, the learning curve was quick.

Now, as we relax for the evening in the midst of the forest, I find I can breathe again. We've put many miles between us and Hassan and after continuing to push ourselves further and further away from him for close to four hours, I'm quite sure we've lost him.

"We are safe here," I say as I give Bowie a reassuring smile.

Meanwhile, Jack has seen to collecting various twigs and branches from the forest floor and lights a flame on the end of his index finger, courtesy of his magic. The firewood before us instantly takes.

"Sinbad," Bowie says as she turns to face me. "I didn't ask for your permission before I

222

thrust your soul into Dolion's body, and for that, I'm sorry."

I shake my head as I look at her. "You will never know how deeply grateful I am to you for your quick thinking. You have given me the chance to live again and, most importantly, to hold you like a man can hold a woman."

I then pull Bowie closer to me, holding her tightly, just to enjoy how good she feels against me. Then I give her a deep kiss. It feels so wonderful to touch her, even if it's through another man's hands.

When I feel her tongue in my mouth, I'm suddenly on fire, as hot as a burning ember being stoked into a pure flame. Pleasuring her when I was inside her body was a marvelous experience. But there's no comparison to this— being able to touch her and feel her as a man should. I can now do the one thing I've wanted to do all along—make love to her. And based on the expression in her eyes, she's thinking along the same lines.

I turn to face Jack, who watches us both with curiosity and amusement in his eyes. Whether he stays, goes, or joins in, I care not. All I do care about is feeling myself inside Bowie for the first time ever.

"Don't mind me," Jack says on a chuckle.

I turn to face Bowie then and find her attention already on me. She is ready.

She's not my first lover. As a sailor, I've enjoyed many remarkable women in my lifetime. But none of them are anything like her.

From the moment I first touch her, I predict I will lose control. She has the advantage, and that includes her ability to consume me. She's one of those women a man can never get enough of or stop thinking about. So, I drink her essence in, kissing her as if she's the last woman on earth. For me, she is.

I inhale her scent and she dances freely inside my head, adding more fuel to the already blazing fire. I gently nudge her into the bed of leaves beneath her, being careful to make sure there aren't any rocks or sharp objects beneath her head.

When I lean across her, I lap up the way she feels. Jack remains silent in the background, for which I'm appreciative. It can't be easy to watch what's unfolding, even for a well-seasoned man such as he.

Bowie moans when I trail kisses down her neck, taking my time. The sound she makes is music to my ears.

"It feels so good to finally be together in the flesh," she whispers.

"So good," I murmur between kisses as I pull her toward me again. She moans when I plant my lips on hers, swirling my tongue with hers in a delicious tango that sends electric sparks coursing through my veins and stimulates all my nerves. I tangle my fingers in her soft hair, quickly losing myself in her body as the magma inside me begins to bubble.

Though separated by our bodies, I feel like we're still one person. We're part of one another.

The heat of the moment swiftly evaporates, but the slow-burning embers from deep inside us, our desires, steadily smolder. Everything moves in slow motion when I continue my gentle seduction with my hands, my mouth, and my tongue. I try to memorize every moment and every sensation.

I pause temporarily to look into her eyes. Her nipples brush the coarse hairs on my chest as I continue to kiss her. I slip my hand between her legs, stroking her clit as we continue to dance with our tongues. I can hardly hold myself back.

Another revelation suddenly dawns on me. Before now, when I was still alive, I existed without love for the most part. The women I bedded were just temporary distractions and minor amusements. They appealed to me physically, but never emotionally. I can scarcely remember the last time any woman responded to me with love, until now.

Bowie loves me and I love her and now I'm able to experience her in life. This is a gift and, truly, the best gift I've ever received.

The forest vibrates with the sounds we make, echoing our moans and sighs all around us. She gasps when my mouth moves away from hers, but happily moans when my hands cup her breasts and I kiss them, slowly swirling my tongue around her nipples while I caress them.

Her face is a mask of sheer pleasure as she lies back, loving every moment of us being together. Almost as much as I. My cock is granite-hard, pressing into her thigh as I move downward, peppering little butterfly kisses along her belly until I find her pubic mound. She opens her legs, making herself more available to me, and I continue kissing her thighs as she squirms beneath me anxiously.

I slide further down her body, feeling so at home inside her open legs. I slip my hands beneath her rear cheeks and pull her toward me before I part her wet, moist layers with my tongue. I lap up her juices, the sweetest nectar I've ever tasted.

"Gods, yes!" she squeals as she places both her hands on my head, eagerly guiding me.

I'm savoring every moment we share. Pushing her legs further apart and her hips higher, I ever-so-slowly devour her with my mouth, lips, and tongue. From time to time, I revert to pulling lightly and suckling the swelling bud of her clit with my teeth.

I redouble my efforts until her legs begin to jerk involuntarily, every fiber of her responding to me. Her nails gouge into my back as I tongue-fuck her, using my fingers to massage her sweet spot until I grant her the release she's so desperate for. Her body quakes as the force of a massive orgasm devolves into smaller ones. And I milk every single one of them.

I pull her sideways and lifting one of her legs, impale her with one fluid thrust. I pump her slowly, in and out, never taking my eyes off hers.

My large cock pulsates inside her, rubbing and filling her up. I pull her upward, lifting her legs over my shoulders, and drive myself so deep inside her, she whimpers.

"Gods, I'm ready to come," I suddenly moan, unable to restrain myself any longer. I explode before we disentangle and then I have to lie down beside her to catch my breath. I lift my head to look at her, smiling as I push away a tendril of hair that falls across her face.

"I love you so much, Bowie."

"I love you too, Sinbad," she replies sleepily.

"That was quite… entertaining," Jack says from where he stands a ways off, watching us. As I turn to face him, I realize he's shed his clothing and holds his cock in his hands, stroking it in long, slow pulls.

"Come," I say as I spread Bowie's legs so they're facing him.

He doesn't wait for another invitation but instantly hurries over to her and she welcomes him with outstretched arms.

The afterglow of our lovemaking still burns brightly from within me. Everything feels so right with the world, even if it's a fleeting moment.

Jack

I lean closer and kiss her, covering her sweet

mouth with mine, letting my animal instincts take over. Slowly, we explore one another with our mouths. I'm hungry for her, even starving, as I've imagined this exact situation more times than I can count.

We eagerly entangle our tongues, and I savor her taste. I don't think I've ever wanted a woman as much as I do Bowie. And I know she wants me too. I can feel it, see it in her eyes. Pulling away from her mouth, I pepper little kisses downward, planting more on her collarbone.

She gasps when my mouth covers her left nipple, licking and sucking until she moans. Her fingers coil tunnels through my hair, pulling me closer.

I take my time, watching her reactions when I caress her. I slip my hand beneath her thighs, examining her slender legs with my fingers until I reach the slick folds between her legs. She's already very hot and wet, owing to Sinbad, of course. I slip one finger inside her eager hole, massaging her folds, lapping up the way she arches her back toward me while I gently finger-fuck her.

"I want you deep inside me," she whispers, pulling my face close to hers in another heated kiss.

I pull her toward me and flip her over so she's now on her hands and knees. Then, spreading her legs open, I continue to slip my fingers inside her. I slide them in and out of her slippery folds while my cock rests between the perfectly round globes of her ass. Nothing matters to me but this moment as I hungrily prepare to enter her.

But Bowie has her own ideas. She pulls away from me and, pushing me down, climbs atop me. And I invite her to climb on top of me. I hold on to her waist with both hands and begin sliding her up and down the length of my cock, thrilling every time I hit the spot that launches any woman into dramatic ecstasy. I wait for that precious moment, getting her off before I join her. And joining her isn't far off. I can't help it—I've wanted her for so long and to feel her now, it's too much to resist.

I flip her to her back, then pull her upward, wrapping her legs around my waist before impaling her again. I slide her body up and down as I fuck her in hard, deep strokes. Her cries of delight echo through the forest and I'm beyond pleased that Hassan is nowhere nearby. My thrusts become more deliberate as she grows animated, begging and squealing. I respond by giving it to her long, hard, and fast, until she erupts into one long, continuous moan, clutching my back as she climaxes.

I quickly join her, pumping harder and faster while she braces herself with my shoulders, her breasts pressing into my chest and her body shuddering as we both achieve another orgasm together.

Chapter Twenty-Two
Bowie

When we return to the small village where
Morningstar left Claude with a "healer", we scour the
place and eventually find him in the tavern, burying his
remorse in a tankard of ale.

As soon as Claude sees Sinbad, who appears as
Dolion, he throws his tankard aside and unleashes his
blade. I once again must intervene and thankfully,
Claude's willing to accept the explanation of what
happened to Dolion quicker than Jack did.

After dealing with Morningstar and having sex
with both Jack and Sinbad, I'm exhausted. If I hadn't
absorbed the life energy from Morningstar, I don't
know how I'd be fairing now. And, regarding that
subject, I'm not sure how to feel. Honestly, with
everything I've learned about our shared pasts and who
I really am, I'm not sure how I'll ever feel the same
about myself. I'm just... not the person I thought I was.

To distract me from the thoughts going
through my head, which I haven't yet shared
with any of them, mainly because I don't even
know where to start, Claude explains how he

escaped the healer. Of course, the person Morningstar left Claude with wasn't a healer at all, but one of his devoted servants.

"Thanks to whatever potions he kept pouring down my throat," Claude says bitterly, "I spent several days in a deeper fog than that damned spell Dolion, er Morningstar, had us all under."

I squeeze his free hand. "It's good to know you were able to escape."

"Oh, I'd probably still be trapped there if a barmaid hadn't stopped by to show my healer an enjoyable time," Claude says with a chuckle. "That made the bastard forget me long enough so I could escape into the woods. And then I simply stayed out of sight until the potions wore off. Eventually, without Morningstar or the potions addling my brain, things started coming back to me."

Jack puts a brotherly hand on his shoulder. "I was afraid Morningstar killed you outright."

"Strange, don't you think, that he chose not to?" Sinbad asks, stroking his chin. "I can't help but wonder if he had uglier plans for all of us?"

"Sinbad raises a good point," I say. "Morningstar did a real number on all of us."

After everyone agrees with that statement, I swallow and tell them the truth about who I am, worried all the while that they'll reject me as soon as they realize I was, long ago,

Morningstar's mate. "If you choose to leave me, I understand," I offer, my voice dropping because the truth is that I love all of them and I hope they'll decide to stay with me, even though I'm not the woman they thought I was.

I feel a light smack on the top of my head and turn to see Jack scowling at me.

"Don't be a silly fool," he says with a laugh. "I trained you better than that."

"I just want to be understanding, given the shock about who I am," I explain as I look from him to the rest of them. "And I would understand if any of you stopped loving me… because of that."

Jack continues to frown at me. "And I'm trying to make you understand that any falsehoods on our journey had nothing to do with you."

"Everything else was real," Claude affirms. "At least, for me it was." He takes a deep breath. "And regardless of who you were in a past life, you are and always will be Bowie to me."

"Perhaps I'm speaking out of turn," Sinbad interjects. "But I believe I speak for all of us when I say we all love you, and we wish to stay with you no matter what."

"Yes," Claude says and nods. "I second that."

"Me too," Jack adds. "Each of us would go

to the ends of the world to protect you, and this doesn't change that. Nothing could."

I feel tears well in my eyes. "Then none of you are angry with me?"

Jack raises both of his eyebrows in genuine surprise. "Angry for what?"

"For falling in love with Morningstar," I reply as I shake my head, trying to understand where the old me ends and the new me begins. "As much as I hate to admit it, there's still a part of me that loves him."

"Of course, we aren't mad with you, Bowie," Claude says, stroking my cheek. "Morningstar lied to you, manipulated you, and made you think he deserved your love."

I shake my head. "But now that I know the truth, I shouldn't still love him. Yet... I do."

"Love can't magically disappear," Sinbad counters, but it's Dolion's face I see. It's a difficult thing to recognize the fact that Dolion is now Sinbad. It's like having the two men I fell in love with rolled up into one. I can only wonder where the real Dolion's soul might be. When things settle down, I fully intend to find out. I can't let that poor man's soul wander around lost. I need to ensure his soul was reaped.

"It took time for you to fall in love with Morningstar," Jack continues. "And it will take more time for you to stop loving him."

233

I think back to my conversations with Morningstar, and all the endearments he showered on me. "You know, I think he did love me… in his own way."

"No," Jack says with finality, shaking his head. "Whatever else he may be, Morningstar is an evil, power-hungry despot who cares only about his own selfish needs. True love doesn't include disguises and manipulation, which are exactly the things he used to deceive you."

"We love you," Claude adds before kissing my cheek.

Sinbad gets on his haunches to lean closer. "Now and always."

It's too much to bear at once: the truth about my past, their unconditional forgiveness, their love, and Morningstar's exposure. I grab each one and kiss him softly on the lips, letting them know my love for them is still as real as it ever was.

My nerves are on edge when I stand before the Guild.

Having just confessed my crimes against them, I wonder what will happen to me now. They may decide to lock me away forever, along with Jack and Claude. Since Sinbad was no more than a phantom and didn't actually commit any crimes, he's already deemed innocent in Guild's eyes. But Sinbad stands in solidarity with the three of us, ready to face our sentences and stay by our sides.

"While what you have done is heinous beyond words," the magistrate announces from his bench, "we have all borne witness to Morningstar's power all too well. You could never have taken so many souls at once without his wicked trickery and deceit."

"Yes," I say meekly, waiting for the other shoe to drop.

"In light of the guilt we know you already suffer, it is the sentence of this court that you shall retrieve every soul you extracted and return it to its rightful owner."

"What?" I gasp, amazed they aren't imprisoning me or ordering my death but, at the same time, what they're asking is near impossible. "But how can I do that? Their bodies will have surely decomposed by now."

"We will aid you with their preservation," the magistrate replies. "Briar Rose will prevent their bodies from putrefying. Once she restores them, you may return their souls. Will that repair all the damage you have done?"

"Yes," I say. "Yes, it will. I'll be very happy to do that. Thank you."

"She should retrieve Andric first," another member of the council says, causing the others to murmur amongst themselves.

"Andric?" I repeat.

The magistrate nods and holds up his hand for silence before addressing me again. "Aria needs him to reign over Delerood and bring his armies into battle. He is our biggest priority, hence, he has now become your biggest priority, as well."

"I understand."

"You agree to make this journey, then?"

"I do. I'll return the souls of everyone I slayed."

"See that you do! We shall discuss your future status after you have finished serving your sentence."

"Thank you," I repeat, stepping back so Jack and Claude can be sentenced for their crimes.

Fortunately, their offenses are quickly dismissed. They're forgiven for their part in the conflict in exchange for their loyal assistance to the Guild, something they both immediately promise.

Although I don't discuss it with my men, my heart still aches for the loss of Morningstar, much though I hate it. I don't know how much damage I did to him before he managed to push me away. At the time, I was prepared to wring out all of his strength. In a way, I'm glad I failed. I never wanted to kill him, not truly. It's an unfortunate part of being tied to him in another life—I'm still tied to him in this one, at least partially.

I can't imagine not loving him, but now that I know what he is and what he's capable of, I sincerely hope, when the time comes that I face him again, I'll make the right choice.

You will make the right choice, Bowie, I tell myself. *No matter the history between you and*

236

Morningstar, he is evil and you are good. You will make the right choice for yourself and for your men. You will make the right choice for the Guild and all of Fantasia.

Chapter Twenty-Three
Sinbad

I don't expect I can enter the ether now that
I've borrowed a human body.

But it turns out not to be an obstacle. I
merely leave Dolion's body sleeping in bed
before Bowie and I enter the otherworld to
search for Andric.

This place is not at all as fearsome as I
expected it to be.

It turns out the ether is divided into separate
places, each designed exclusively for the people
who congregate there. There are areas designed
just for children—giant playgrounds with lots of
sweets, games, puppies and kittens. There are
other places for musicians and artists and
athletes. Anything that binds people together
probably has an area somewhere in the ether
reserved only for them.

The people I find in the Endless Night are
quite lively for being deceased. This place is
peaceful and happy. No one complains as they
go about their daily afterlives. No one seems

scared, cold or hungry either. There's no fear or pain. Whatever ailed them in their human existence seems to be cured in this one.

Among the souls dwelling here are those of a more elevated status: faeries, wizards, witches, and even self-proclaimed gods. Everything that dies appears to come here.

Each location leads us to another place. Eventually, we enter a swirling kaleidoscope of color and find ourselves in a quiet area where the white sands meet a crystal-clear ocean. Along the shore, I see tables filled with delicious meats and seafood, tropical fruits and any kind of drink one can imagine. People relax on the endless beaches, enjoying the fresh air and warm sun rays that beat down on them. Everything here feels real, but Bowie insists it isn't.

"None of this exists except in our imagination," she explains. "Nothing is like what we think it is outside the ether. These places continue to change and grow as more people join them, each making his or her own subtle additions."

"Suppose someone arrives with a less-than-desirable change to contribute?"

"People here don't care about that, not the way humans do. They aren't even people here, really, more like entities—spirits, souls. They aren't jealous or petty. All their emotions reside only in the mortal world. If anyone decides their selected place in the ether no longer suits them, they can always relocate, as long as they don't go outside the afterlife."

A sense of alarm bolts through me. "So, once a soul crosses the Edge of Endless Night, they can never return?"

"Don't worry, Sinbad. You're not trapped here—not after I gave you life again in Dolion's body."

"Speaking of which," I say with a bit of guilt. "Do you believe Morningstar killed Dolion? And will we find his original soul here?"

"Yes, Morningstar killed him," she says with confidence. "Since I didn't reap him, he most likely found his own way here."

"I wonder if his name is still Dolion," I muse.

"We may never know," she mutters. Then she looks up at me and adds, "But for now, that body is called Sinbad and we both have more important things to concern ourselves with."

Looking around, I don't know why I was so resistant to coming here. I could have relaxed on this very beach with a schooner of ale in my hand. Bowie walks beside me, and I'm in my own paradise whenever I'm with her.

We press on and pass through a forest filled with souls who dedicated their lives to the Earth

Mother. Now they exist as the very things they once tried to save. To some, it would be rather restrictive, but they find comfort in it.

I notice a long line of fisherman sitting in beach chairs on the shore. Each contentedly waits for a fish to take their bait. I see several reeling in their catches and quickly releasing the fish back into the water. I wonder how many souls inhabit those waters and what it might be like to spend an eternity just swimming about in the depths of the ocean.

My thoughts are interrupted when one of the fisherman storms angrily toward us. As he gets closer, I realize he's Andric. He was fishing quietly on the beach and seems more bored than happy. At least, until he spotted us. The moment he does, he's instantly on his feet, his temples pulsing angrily as he bears down on Bowie.

"You!" he yells at her. "You're a shepherdess!"

"Yes," she says, standing still without flinching as he approaches her.

"You are one of those who forced us into the place!" he demands.

"I am and I'm also the one who has come to remove you and return you to the land of the living," she explains.

Andric doesn't respond as vehemently. "You know that isn't allowed."

"It is now," Bowie replies. "The Guild

approved it. Well, they demanded it, actually. Anyway, they need you in Delerood, so they sent me to find you."

Andric nods. "Very good, I've tarried here long enough!"

"Is there no one you wish to say goodbye to?" I ask.

"Like who? The fucking fish? I think they'll manage without me." Then he grunts. "I assume we're digging up my corpse?"

"Not exactly," I answer as Andric looks at me narrowly.

"Didn't get your name, sailor," he says, squinting at me.

"Sinbad," I reply, watching the look of surprise on his face.

"I met a Sinbad once, but that was a long time ago," he says. "You look nothing like him."

"You aren't the only one who's been treated to an out-of-body experience," Bowie says carefully.

"Well, if you're the same sailor I knew, I'd keep that body if I were you."

"You're pretty amusing for a dead man."

"Takes one to know one," Andric retorts.

All of us laugh, glad for some levity, even for a moment.

Bowie summons the soul of a Roc, and the two of us ride him back to Delerood. Once we emerge with Andric, we drop his soul into his body, which was prepared ahead of time by Briar Rose.

I sigh. "One down, and just over three thousand to go."

Epilogue
Bowie

Each night, I have the same dream—
Morningstar making love to me.

Tonight, the dream is particularly vivid, as
if he's actually here beside me. All the lives I've
lived with him blur in my mind, flashing in bits
and pieces.

Even in the dream, I'm aware of the
tragedy we suffered. He never foresaw whom I
would embrace in my personage as Bowie. He
also had no idea I would forsake *him* in order to
save *them*. The worst part for me, however, is I
can't forget him. He's part of me, even though
he's also my nemesis and a monster.

*Images of him fill my brain. I see myself
standing with him in my former beauty before
he cast me into the shepherdess I am now. I see
us clearly and I know it's not a dream, but a
memory, one of many that regularly returns.*

*In the memory, Morningstar removes his shirt, and
his large body ripples with muscles. I don't fail to
notice all the scars that crisscross his abdomen, some*

even wrapping around his sides. When I look into his eyes, I'm reminded of the first time I saw him, when he removed the mask of Dolion and revealed his true self. I was aghast, finding him hideous, and now I can't recollect why. When I think of Morningstar now, I believe he's beautiful. This must be Asharah's response to him and not Bowie's.

Regardless, his scars are the evidence of the punishments he endured by the people who refused to let him exist in their countries. The violence generally took the form of beatings, whippings, and sometimes, worse. Despite his power, we went to places where gods stronger than him cast us out mercilessly.

I never mention the scars, as the experiences are too painful for him to recall. He hates to be reminded of his failures–or his shame.

Footsteps sound nearby, and he grabs my hand to hide us in the woods. Men rush past us, but we're safely hidden behind the shrubs at the edge of the forest.

"We have to get out of here," he whispers. "They'll be back in no time."

"Shouldn't we stay and fight?" I ask.

"No, not here. We're outnumbered, and I won't risk your safety. This is no place for us. We will have to find another."

I wake up in a total panic, and the vivid reality of the dream takes my breath away. Jack stirs, but I turn away from him and cuddle Claude on my other side. Sinbad is also nearby. He's been staying awake all night, for fear someone might come for me.

"Are you all right, Bowie?" he asks me.

"I'm fine," I tell him. "Just another disturbing dream."

"About *him* again?"

"Yes," I reply, deliberately saying no more.

My dreams replay all the excitement Morningstar and I enjoyed in our former life together. They're a reminder of the visceral, animal passion we shared. Apparently, I once thrived on carnage and power as much as he did in those days. That's the essence of our relationship.

But worse than that, the dreams warn me of what I forbid myself to feel. I can't overlook what Morningstar is by allowing our romance from so long ago to overshadow what he is now. He might love me, but he loves power more than anything. And I know he would destroy even that which he loves in order to get more power.

The prophecy poem spells out my place in this battle:

Empress of Eidolon
Death's final decree
Shall battle against the morning
And bring him to his knees.

I am the Empress of Eidolon.

And, as such, I have to live with the knowledge that I must kill the man I love.

246

~

To Be Continued in
BELLE

Now Available!

DOWNLOAD FREE EBOOKS!
It's as easy as:

1. Visit my website (hpmallory.com)

2. Sign up in the popup box or the link on the home page

3. Check your email!

HP MALLORY is a New York Times and
USA Today Bestselling Author!

She lives in Southern California with her son, where
she is at work on her next book.
Be sure to visit her at www.hpmallory.com!

Printed in Great Britain
by Amazon